BRIDGE OVER TROUBLED WATERS

David Bird, creator of the famous Abbot series, is acknowledged as the world's best when it comes to humorous bridge fiction. As the bridge cruise traverses the Far East, the bridge organiser, Richard Knight, visits Pat Pong – the notorious red-light district of Bangkok – and is enticed by three attractive Thai girls into a bridge game. Other hilarious adventures take place in a drug den in Hong Kong, in backpacker-land in Bali, in a Shinto monastery in Kyoto and in the Double Bay Club in Sydney.

David Bird's army of followers will know what to expect: a mixture of top-class bridge, exhilarating narrative and a host of true-to-life comic characters.

BRIDGE OVER TROUBLED WATERS

David Bird

IN ASSOCIATION WITH

PETER CRAWLEY

First published in Great Britain 2002
in association with Peter Crawley
by Cassell & Co

Second impression published 2017
in association with Peter Crawley
by Weidenfeld & Nicolson
a division of the Orion Publishing Group Ltd
Carmelite House, 50 Victoria Embankment
London EC4Y 0DZ

An Hachette UK Company

A CIP catalogue record for this book is available from the British Library.

ISBN 978 0 304 36115 1

Printed in Great Britain by
CPI Group (UK) Ltd, Croydon CR0 4YY

FSC
www.fsc.org

www.orionbooks.co.uk

CONTENTS

1
Departure from India

The cruise ship *King Harald II* had left India far behind and was making good speed towards Thailand. Rupert Knight, the bridge organiser, had mixed feelings about the next stage of the world cruise. One or two awkward customers, who had booked only for the England-India segment, had flown back to England. Against that, Jonathan Parker and Mark Rufus were still on board. It was totally absurd that two such expert players should participate in a bridge cruise. A persistent thorn in his side they were, pointing out so many irrelevant errors in his bridge lectures and constantly finishing ahead of him in the sessions.

Knight consulted the fake gold Rolex he had bought in a Bombay market. Five minutes to two! Time to head for the bridge room.

'Ah, there you are, Mr Knight,' said Norma McBain, a 60-year-old Scotswoman. 'We need an adjusted score from yesterday's game, I'm afraid.'

Knight blinked. An adjusted score? The old dears had left it a bit late, hadn't they?

'Yes,' said Ailsa Reid. 'That young man over there...' she leaned towards Knight, lowering her voice to a whisper, 'he hesitated against us.'

'You should have called me at the time, ladies,' Knight replied. 'I could have sorted it out for you then.' He looked around at the various tables, which were gradually filling with players. 'Take your seats. please!'

Norma McBain grabbed hold of Knight's sleeve. 'You mean you're going to let him get away with it?' she demanded. 'We didn't call you at the time because we thought we'd be nowhere near the master points.'

Ailsa Reid nodded. 'As it happens, we were fourth in our line, only a few points behind third.'

'It's far too late to deal with any claimed hesitation, I'm afraid,' said Knight. 'There's one North-South seat left for you, if you're quick.'

Still muttering to themselves, the two Scotswomen headed across the room.

Oakley Hampton, an eccentric American who played bridge in a Minnesota Vikings football shirt, approached Knight. 'I don't seem to have a pardner, tonight,' he said.

That's a surprise, thought Knight. You'd expect a large queue to form to partner such a hopeless player. He looked round desperately for some other unattended player. No such luck, unfortunately. He would have to perform the duty himself.

Play started and this was an early board at their table:

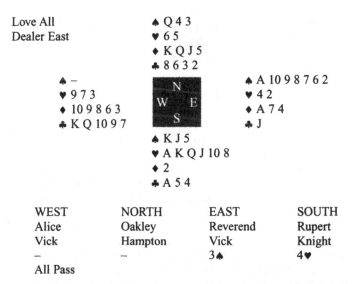

Love All
Dealer East

	♠ Q 4 3		
	♥ 6 5		
	♦ K Q J 5		
	♣ 8 6 3 2		

♠ —   ♠ A 10 9 8 7 6 2
♥ 9 7 3   ♥ 4 2
♦ 10 9 8 6 3   ♦ A 7 4
♣ K Q 10 9 7 ♣ J

♠ K J 5
♥ A K Q J 10 8
♦ 2
♣ A 5 4

WEST	NORTH	EAST	SOUTH
Alice	Oakley	Reverend	Rupert
Vick	Hampton	Vick	Knight
–	–	3♠	4♥
All Pass			

Alice Vick, who was wearing one of her endless collection of floral print dresses, led ♦ 10 against Knight's heart game. Gordon Vick, a retired clergyman, won dummy's king with the ace and paused to consider his return. How many spades did Alice hold? She could hardly have a singleton in the suit he had bid or she would have led it. Perhaps she was void in spades. He could play ace and another spade in that case, giving her a ruff, but if declarer held the club ace he would then have ten tricks. Yes, everything seemed to point towards a club switch being the best idea.

Knight won the jack of clubs switch with the ace and drew trumps in three rounds, East throwing a diamond. What now? Even if East's ♣J was a singleton, prospects were poor. If he tried his luck with the king and jack of spades, seeking an entry to dummy's diamond winners, East would surely hold up the ace for two rounds. After winning the third round, he would then be able to exit safely with a fourth spade.

Suddenly Knight spotted another possibility. He played a fourth round of trumps, East throwing his last diamond. This position had been reached:

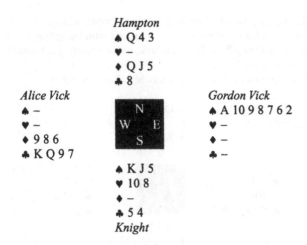

Hampton
♠ Q 4 3
♥ –
♦ Q J 5
♣ 8

Alice Vick
♠ –
♥ –
♦ 9 8 6
♣ K Q 9 7

Gordon Vick
♠ A 10 9 8 7 6 2
♥ –
♦ –
♣ –

♠ K J 5
♥ 10 8
♦ –
♣ 5 4
Knight

Casually Knight played a fifth round of trumps. West and the dummy discarded a club and it was now the Reverend Vick's turn to play. Not giving the matter much thought, he discarded ♠2. Knight was exultant. This was just the card he had been hoping to see. He led ♠5 from his hand, calling for dummy's three. Vick won with the six and then had to cash the ace of spades. Knight unblocked the king from his hand and won the next round with dummy's queen. His two club losers were thrown on dummy's good diamonds and the game had been made.

'I didn't expect to make two spade tricks there,' observed Gordon Vick. 'Still, I suppose it worked out well for you in the end.'

Against many pairs on the cruise, Knight would have pointed out how the contract could have been beaten. If the Reverend Vick had retained his ♠2, he could have allowed South's ♠5 to win. He would then have been able to keep declarer out of the dummy. The Vicks were a pleasant couple, though, one of the few not to make any complaints during the cruise. There was no point in upsetting them, waving good-bye to a favourable comment sheet at the end of the voyage.

Oakley Hampton leaned towards the clergyman. 'Couldn't you beat that one?' he said. 'You should keep the two of spades. You had plenty of other spades to throw.'

Alice Vick eyed Hampton disapprovingly. What a vulgar man he was! How could he wear that dreadful purple sports shirt when most of the players were attired in evening dress? Not that there was any sense in his present rantings. If Gordon could have beaten the contract, he would have done. It was only a matter of weeks since she and Gordon had won the Gladys Beaming Vase, a prized trophy at the Worthing

Bridge Club. Still, perhaps she should give the American the benefit of the doubt. He might not have heard about that.

Halfway through the evening duplicate, with their score hovering around the 45% mark, Knight and his partner met the cruise's star performers, Jonathan Parker and Mark Rufus.

```
North-South game        ♠ 7 5 4
Dealer North            ♥ A 5 3 2
                        ♦ A K 9 6 3
                        ♣ A
        ♠ J 10 9 2          N          ♠ Q 3
        ♥ –             W       E       ♥ J 10 9 7 6
        ♦ Q J 10 2          S          ♦ 8 7 4
        ♣ Q 10 8 4 2                   ♣ K 6 5
                        ♠ A K 8 6
                        ♥ K Q 8 4
                        ♦ 5
                        ♣ J 9 7 3
```

WEST	NORTH	EAST	SOUTH
Rupert	Jonathan	Oakley	Mark
Knight	Parker	Hampton	Rufus
–	1♦	Pass	1♥
Pass	4♣	Pass	4NT
Pass	5♣	Pass	6♥
Pass	Pass	Double	All Pass

A splinter-bid sequence carried Mark Rufus to a small slam in hearts and the American lost no time in doubling this contract. Knight, who was on lead, stared down at his cards. Had Hampton heard of the Lightner Double? It was unlikely. He knew little else about the game and was probably doubling on a trump stack. Still, it was surely best to lead a diamond, dummy's suit, just in case Hampton had done something sensible for a change.

Rufus won the queen of diamonds lead with dummy's ace and called for a low trump. Hampton considered the matter for a moment, then inserted the nine of trumps. Rufus won with the king and West showed out, discarding a club.

Rufus nodded thoughtfully for a few moments, then crossed to the ace of clubs and threw a spade on the diamond king. A diamond ruff was followed by a club ruff and declarer's two top spades. A second club ruff put the lead in dummy, with these cards still to be played:

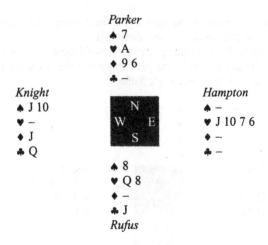

Parker
- ♠ 7
- ♥ A
- ♦ 9 6
- ♣ –

Knight
- ♠ J 10
- ♥ –
- ♦ J
- ♣ Q

Hampton
- ♠ –
- ♥ J 10 7 6
- ♦ –
- ♣ –

- ♠ 8
- ♥ Q 8
- ♦ –
- ♣ J

Rufus

'Play a diamond,' said Mark Rufus.

There was nothing Oakley Hampton could do. If he ruffed low, declarer would overruff with the eight and score his last two trumps separately. The American eventually decided to ruff high, with the 10, but Rufus overruffed with the queen and ruffed his last club with the ace. The lead of dummy's last diamond allowed him to score his ♥8 en passant and the slam had been made.

Oakley Hampton shook his head in disbelief. 'I had two certain trump tricks,' he exclaimed, spreading his hand face-up on the table. 'Look, jack-ten-nine fifth!'

Knight feigned sympathy as he surveyed his partner's hand. Without the foolish double he would indeed have scored two trump tricks. He could have played low on the first round of trumps, with no reason to expect declarer to finesse the eight.

Hampton glanced to his right, seeing a column of 650s on the score-sheet. 'The double didn't cost, fortunately,' he said. 'Minus 1430 would have been a bottom, anyway.'

Knight maintained an impassive expression. What about the plus 100 that they should have scored? Would that not have picked up the odd match-point or two?

Knight could not believe it when Rufus ended in another slam on the very next board. Was there any law against him holding a few high cards himself?

Game All   ♠ A K J 5 4
Dealer East   ♥ K Q J 10 6
                 ♦ 4
                 ♣ 8 7

♠ 9 7 6		♠ 3 2
♥ 7	N	♥ 8 5 4 3
♦ K 7	W E	♦ Q 10 9 8 3
♣ K J 10 6 5 3 2	S	♣ Q 4

                 ♠ Q 10 8
                 ♥ A 9 2
                 ♦ A J 6 5 2
                 ♣ A 9

WEST	NORTH	EAST	SOUTH
Rupert	Jonathan	Oakley	Mark
Knight	Parker	Hampton	Rufus
–		–Pass	1NT
Pass	2♥	Pass	2♠
Pass	3♥	Pass	3♠
Pass	4NT	Pass	5♣
Pass	5♦	Pass	5NT
Pass	7♠	All Pass	

'Partner's 3♥ was forcing to game,' said Rufus, 'so my 3♠ was a stronger move than 4♠. 4NT was Roman Key-card. 5♦ asked for the trump queen and my 5NT showed it, but no side-suit king.'

Rupert Knight nodded. Had he asked about the bidding? It was typical of these aspiring young players to show off about their system. Still, if one thing was obvious, it was his opening lead. Any card but a trump would be an absurd gamble.

Rufus won the trump lead in his hand, with the eight, and decided to play for three ruffs in the long trump hand. The ace of diamonds was followed by a diamond ruff with the jack. Although it was only Trick 4, the key moment of the hand had been reached. If declarer crossed to his hand with a trump to take a second diamond ruff, West would beat the contract by throwing his singleton heart. Rufus made no such mistake. His next move was a heart to the ace. After a second diamond ruff with the king, a trump to the 10 permitted a third diamond ruff, with the bare ace. Rufus then returned to the ace of clubs and drew the last trump. 'They're all there now,' he said. 'I can throw my last two losers on dummy's hearts.'

Knight muttered a swear-word under his breath. Another complete zero, you could bank on it, and there was absolutely nothing he could have done about it!

'You had only one heart did you?' queried Rufus.

'Yes, just the one,' replied Knight.

'Heart lead beats it, then,' declared Rufus. 'It kills one of the entries to my hand.'

'Jeez!' exclaimed Hampton. 'You didn't lead a singleton against a slam? You're meant to be the bridge expert here, aren't you?'

'Club lead beats it, too, Mark,' observed Parker. 'Kills one of your entries, just the same.'

Oakley Hampton glared across the table. 'No wonder we never do well together,' he declared. 'Can't even get a good score when they bid too high.'

'A trump lead was obvious from my hand,' declared Knight. He turned towards Rufus, seeking support. 'What would you have led, Mark?'

With a mischievous air Rufus studied the West curtain card. 'Difficult one, isn't it?' he said. 'To tell the truth, I really don't know. It's so close between a heart and a club.'

'I'd lead the singleton every time,' said Hampton. 'In our bridge group back in Minnesota that's one of our Golden Rules.'

Knight sat back wearily in his chair. There seemed to be rather a lot of Golden Rules, back in Minnesota. It was amazing that Hampton remembered them all, in fact. He could never remember which cards had gone.

The next round saw Knight facing the two Scotswomen.

'It's very cold in here,' said Ailsa Reid. 'Just because we're in the Tropics, it doesn't mean that they should overdo the air conditioning.'

Knight smiled politely. He had never met such a pair of moaners. Only last night they had complained that it was too hot.

'Perhaps a nice top will warm us up,' suggested Norma McBain.

Not if I can help it, thought Knight. This was the next board:

East-West game
Dealer South

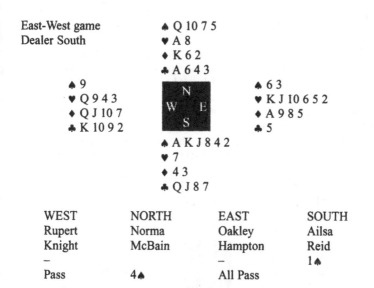

♠ Q 10 7 5
♥ A 8
♦ K 6 2
♣ A 6 4 3

♠ 9
♥ Q 9 4 3
♦ Q J 10 7
♣ K 10 9 2

♠ 6 3
♥ K J 10 6 5 2
♦ A 9 8 5
♣ 5

♠ A K J 8 4 2
♥ 7
♦ 4 3
♣ Q J 8 7

WEST	NORTH	EAST	SOUTH
Rupert	Norma	Oakley	Ailsa
Knight	McBain	Hampton	Reid
–		–	1♠
Pass	4♠	All Pass	

The Scotswomen bid briskly to a game in spades and Knight led ♦Q.
Ailsa Reid called for dummy's king of diamonds, not thinking much of
her luck when this lost to the ace. The defenders persisted with diamonds
and she ruffed the third round. Ace of hearts and a heart ruff eliminated
that suit and she then drew trumps in two rounds, with the ace and queen.

When a club was played to the queen, Knight had a complete count
of the hand. Realising that he would be endplayed if he won with the
club king, he followed smoothly with the two. Ailsa Reid raised her
eyes despairingly to the ceiling. Typical! She does a clever elimination
play, to guard against a 4-1 club break, and the king turns out to be
onside all along. No-one in the whole room would go down, with the
cards lying so favourably. She led a disgruntled ♣7 from her hand, covered by West's ten. 'Ace, please,' she said.

The tall, thin Scotswoman could not believe it when East showed out,
throwing a heart. It then dawned on her that she had two club tricks to
lose. The contract was one down.

Oakley Hampton was less than appreciative of Knight's fine defence.
'Why on earth didn't you win declarer's queen of clubs with the king?'
he demanded. 'I might have had the jack over here.'

'If I win with the king, I'm endplayed,' Knight replied. 'The ♣10
goes to South's jack and she can lead the 8-7 through my 9. Ailsa played
the hand very well. Leading towards the queen was a perfect safety play
against a 4-1 club break either way.'

Norma McBain looked puzzled. 'But clubs were 4-1,' she said, 'and she went down.'

'Yes, it was difficult for you, Ailsa,' continued Knight. 'You needed to allow my ♣10 to win the second round, holding off dummy's ace. If East has another club, the suit must be 3-2. If he doesn't, I will be endplayed.'

With an irritated wave of the hand, Ailsa Reid beckoned for the next board to be put in position. 'That's the way I would have played it,' she said, 'if I wasn't half frozen to death.'

The last round of the evening saw the arrival of the elegantly attired Suchermans. Ralph Sucherman reached a tricky spade game on this deal:

East-West game
Dealer East

♠ 8 3
♥ K 7 3 2
♦ J 8 4
♣ K 6 3 2

♠ 7 4
♥ A J 10 8
♦ A K 9 7 5 3 2
♣ —

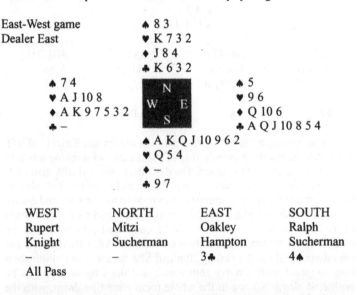

♠ 5
♥ 9 6
♦ Q 10 6
♣ A Q J 10 8 5 4

♠ A K Q J 10 9 6 2
♥ Q 5 4
♦ —
♣ 9 7

WEST	NORTH	EAST	SOUTH
Rupert	Mitzi	Oakley	Ralph
Knight	Sucherman	Hampton	Sucherman
—	—	3♣	4♠
All Pass			

Knight could not make up his mind whether to pass, double 4♠, or bid 5♦. On a bad day the latter bid might well cost 500 or so, with no game on for the opponents. In the end he decided to pass.

'Well, I can't say anything after a hesitation like that,' declared Hampton. 'I pass too.'

For a second Knight closed his eyes. How could Hampton even think of bidding again after opening with a pre-empt? The Minnesota school must rate it quite commonplace to open 3♣, then sacrifice in 5♣ opposite a silent partner.

Knight led the ace of diamonds and Sucherman ruffed. The ace of trumps was followed by a trump to the table's eight and a second diamond ruff. At Trick 5 he led the queen of hearts from his hand. Knight could not afford to hold up or declarer would score two heart tricks. He won with the ace and exited with the jack of hearts.

The key moment had been reached. If hearts had started 3-3, declarer would have to duck this trick, preserving the heart king as an entry to the long card in the suit. Seeking a clue to the heart position, Sucherman considered the lie of the diamonds. The diamond queen had not yet surfaced. If West held A-K-Q to eight diamonds, along with the heart ace, he would surely have tried his luck in Five Diamonds. It looked as if the diamond queen must be with East, which would give him 1-2-3-7 shape. 'King of hearts, please,' said Sucherman.

Declarer ruffed dummy's last diamond, pleased to see the queen appear from East. These cards now remained:

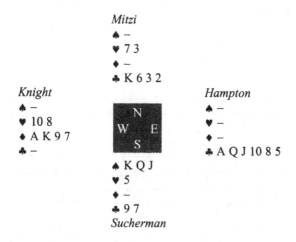

Mitzi
♠ –
♥ 7 3
♦ –
♣ K 6 3 2

Knight
♠ –
♥ 10 8
♦ A K 9 7
♣ –

Hampton
♠ –
♥ –
♦ –
♣ A Q J 10 8 5

Sucherman
♠ K Q J
♥ 5
♦ –
♣ 9 7

Sucherman ran ♣9 to East's 10 and was soon enjoying a heart discard on dummy's ♣K. The spade game had been made.

Mitzi gazed admiringly across the table. 'Such a nice play you make there, Ralph!' she exclaimed. 'It must be good for us. They had a cheap sacrifice in diamonds.'

Hampton reached for his partner's curtain card. 'Five Diamonds was on ice!' he cried. 'You didn't notice you had ace-king seventh in diamonds?'

For a brief moment Knight was tempted to make some barbed reply. No, his role as the cruise bridge organiser would not permit it. The clients' questionnaires, at the end of the cruise, would determine whether any further lucrative cruise jobs came his way. Whatever the provocation, he must exude pleasantness at all times.

Knight contorted his face into a smile. 'Sorry, Oakley,' he said.

2
An Afternoon in Pat Pong

The *King Harald II* had docked at the small port of Laem Chabang on the West coast of Thailand and the passengers had disembarked to join a party of coaches for the two-hour drive to Bangkok. A tour of the Royal Palace and the more important temples was to be the main attraction there. Rupert Knight had a different - and for him, more exciting - objective. He would spend the available time in the bars of Pat Pong, the notorious red light area.

'We have to leave at seven o'clock, whether you're back or not,' warned the driver of Coach 'D'.

'Yes, yes, I'll be back in time,' Knight replied. 'I'm not very interested in temples. I'd much rather spend some time er... on the river and up the klongs.'

Knight was soon in a tuk-tuk, one of the motorised two-wheelers that ply their trade across the city. He held a handkerchief to his face, to protect him from the exhaust fumes coming from all directions. 'You like see special show in Pat Pong?' shouted the tuk-tuk driver, weaving dangerously from one lane to another. 'I know best show. Many, many girls, very pretty. Ping-pong, blowpipe dart, snake, opening coke bottle. Very good show, very cheap. I take you there.'

'No, thank you,' replied Knight firmly. 'I can find my own way around.'

Knight was soon walking along one of the two parallel streets of Pat Pong. Market stalls loaded with all sorts of counterfeit goods filled the roadway. Bars lined the pavements, their music filling the air.

Suddenly Knight found that he was not alone. A teen-aged Thai girl was walking alongside him. 'You American?' she asked.

Knight could not believe his luck. He had rarely seen such an attractive girl. 'I'm from England,' he replied.

'I like England men the best,' the girl declared, taking his arm. 'You here on business?'

'In a way, I suppose,' Knight replied. 'I'm a professional bridge player. I run the bridge on a big cruise ship. I'm just here for the day.'

'Ah, card game bridge!' said the girl excitedly. 'Me and my friends, we just learning.' Suddenly the girl's eyes lit up. 'You must come meet my friends,' she said. 'Only live in next street. They most honoured to meet professional player of bridge game.'

Knight hesitated for a moment. This wasn't exactly what he had had in mind. Still, the girl was inordinately attractive. What was more, against all the odds, she seemed to like him. 'All right,' he said.

Knight could barely believe it when, just ten minutes later, he found himself involved in a bridge game with three bright-eyed Thai girls. They were playing in one of the back rooms of a first-floor bar, a fan whirring above their heads. In the first rubber he partnered the girl he had met in the street.

'My name Thanomjit Sattarwarhorn,' she said. 'You call me Julie, if you like.'

Knight laughed nervously. 'That would be easier,' he replied.

This was the first deal:

```
Love All              ♠ 7 5 2
Dealer West           ♥ A 9 8
                      ♦ 7 3
                      ♣ K 9 7 6 2
    ♠ J 10 6                          ♠ K 9
    ♥ K 6 5          N                ♥ Q J 10 7 4 3 2
    ♦ K Q 5 4 2   W     E             ♦ 8
    ♣ A 4            S                ♣ J 10 5
                      ♠ A Q 8 4 3
                      ♥ —
                      ♦ A J 10 9 6
                      ♣ Q 8 3
```

WEST	NORTH	EAST	SOUTH
Santhanee	'Julie'	Chalalai	Rupert Knight
1 ♦	Pass	1 ♥	1 ♠
2 ♥	2 ♠	3 ♥	4 ♠
All Pass			

West led ♣A and Julie was somewhat reluctant to display her dummy. 'I not sure you playing the five-card majors,' she said. 'Only have three trumps for you.'

'That's fine,' said Knight. 'My bid was an overcall, so that must show a five-card suit.'

The East player, a girl from Chiang Rai who was darker skinned than the other two, leaned forward. 'That German guy who playing last week, he overcall on 4-card suit. You remember it?'

'That's right,' said her partner, an unusually tall girl for a Thai. 'He overcall One Spade on just ace-king fourth.'

Julie laughed. 'Typical!' she exclaimed. 'Some men think they can do anything when they come to Pat Pong.'

West continued with a second round of clubs and Knight won with the king in dummy, in order to take a trump finesse. A trump to the queen won the trick and he next played the ace of trumps, dropping the king from East. When he continued with the queen of clubs, West decided not to ruff with her master trump. The queen held the trick and Knight then led the jack of diamonds. West won with the diamond queen and the eight fell from East. West cashed her master trump, to leave this position:

'Julie'
♠ –
♥ A 9 8
♦ 7
♣ 9 7

Santhanee
♠ –
♥ K 6
♦ K 5 4 2
♣ –

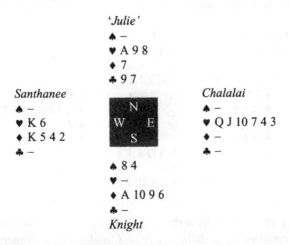

Chalalai
♠ –
♥ Q J 10 7 4 3
♦ –
♣ –

♠ 8 4
♥ –
♦ A 10 9 6
♣ –

Knight

A heart exit would be hopeless, giving declarer access to the dummy and the two good clubs. Santhanee decided to try her luck with a low diamond, wincing when dummy's ♦7 won the trick. Knight proceeded to discard his diamond losers and the contract was made.

'Why you lead low diamond?' cried Chalalai. 'You have nothing higher than dummy's seven?'

Knight assumed his well-practised expert expression. 'Only the king,' he replied. 'If she plays the king, all my diamonds are good.'

Julie smiled admiringly across the table, displaying her perfect white teeth. 'He professional player,' she informed her colleagues. 'We can learn lot from him.'

The next few hands confirmed that the three girls were relative newcomers to the game. Knight then had a chance to land the first rubber.

```
North-South game          ♠ K Q 3
Dealer East               ♥ Q 10 7 2
                          ♦ 10 8 3
                          ♣ K 6 2
        ♠ 9 5 2                          ♠ A J 7 4
        ♥ 9 4            N               ♥ 6
        ♦ Q 7 5 4     W     E            ♦ J 9 6 2
        ♣ Q J 10 7       S               ♣ A 9 5 4
                          ♠ 10 8 6
                          ♥ A K J 8 5 3
                          ♦ A K
                          ♣ 8 3
```

WEST	NORTH	EAST	SOUTH
Santhanee	'Julie'	Chalalai	Rupert Knight
–	–	Pass	1♥
Pass	3♥	Pass	4♥
All Pass			

The queen of clubs was led and Julie's face lit up in another splendid smile. 'You very happy with me this time,' she informed Knight. 'Four-card support in trumps!'

Knight, who was unaccustomed to attractive girls smiling at him, paused to savour the moment. 'Excellent dummy, Julie,' he replied. 'Thanks very much.'

The defenders persisted with clubs and Knight ruffed the third round. He drew one round of trumps with the ace, then took the small risk of cashing his two diamond honours. When both defenders followed suit, he crossed to the trump queen and ruffed dummy's last diamond. These cards remained:

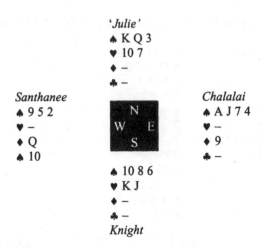

'Julie'
♠ K Q 3
♥ 10 7
♦ —
♣ —

Santhanee
♠ 9 5 2
♥ —
♦ Q
♠ 10

Chalalai
♠ A J 7 4
♥ —
♦ 9
♣ —

♠ 10 8 6
♥ K J
♦ —
♣ —

Knight

When Knight played a spade to the king, the dark-skinned girl from Chiang Rai won with the ace and returned ♠4.

Knight sat back in his chair. Should he play the 10 or the eight? If East had held off the ace, of course, she would have beaten the contract. He would have had to return to hand with a trump and lead a second spade to the queen. The question was: would East be more likely to spot the need to duck if her holding was headed by the ace-jack or the ace-nine? If she held the ace and jack, even a quite moderate player might spot the advantage of ducking.

Concluding that East was more likely to hold the nine than the jack, Knight eventually tried the eight from his hand. The tall Santhanee covered with the nine and the game was one down.

'Hah! Chalalai and me fooling you there!' exclaimed Santhanee. 'You could making it by playing ten instead of eight. Ten wins trick.'

'Yes, you girls play a strong game,' Knight declared. 'You bid very well and you defend very well.'

'Sawaddi ka, sa lae set farang yorm pom,' said an animated Julie to her friends. *'Tam ruat mai mi kone krong chuey duey!'*

'Let me in on the secret,' said Knight. 'What did she say?'

The three girls giggled. 'She say she like you,' Santhanee declared. 'She say also that...'

Julie leapt from her chair and clamped her hand over Santhanee's lips, preventing her from saying any more. 'Santhanee has very big mouth,' she said, laughing prettily. 'Biggest mouth in Pat Pong!'

Chalalai joined in the laughter. *'Gai hor bai toey, bah mee nam mud-sa-gang,'* she said.

Rupert Knight surveyed the scene happily. He hadn't the faintest idea what they were talking about, of course. Perhaps it was better that he didn't know.

This was the next deal:

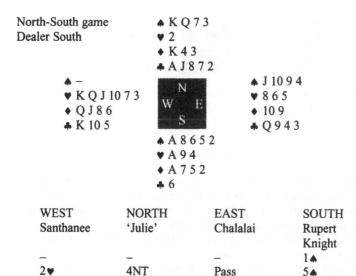

North-South game
Dealer South

♠ K Q 7 3
♥ 2
♦ K 4 3
♣ A J 8 7 2

♠ —
♥ K Q J 10 7 3
♦ Q J 8 6
♣ K 10 5

♠ J 10 9 4
♥ 8 6 5
♦ 10 9
♣ Q 9 4 3

♠ A 8 6 5 2
♥ A 9 4
♦ A 7 5 2
♣ 6

WEST	NORTH	EAST	SOUTH
Santhanee	'Julie'	Chalalai	Rupert Knight
–	–	–	1♠
2♥	4NT	Pass	5♠
Pass	5NT	Pass	6♣
Pass	6♠	All Pass	

Knight won the king of hearts lead with the ace and led a low trump. He groaned inwardly when West showed out, throwing a heart. What appalling luck. It hadn't been totally obvious how to play the hand, even if the trumps broke 2-2. With this 4-0 break, there was surely no hope at all. He would have to lose one trump and at least one diamond.

Chalalai laughed. 'You happy man when Julie hold four trumps,' she said. 'You not so happy when Chalalai hold them!'

Knight decided to ruff as many clubs as he could in the South hand. He won the first round of trumps with dummy's king, cashed the ace of clubs and ruffed a club. A low heart ruff was followed by a club ruff and another low heart ruff, East following suit. After ruffing a third club, Knight cashed the ace and king of diamonds. This was the end position:

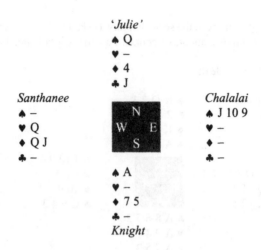

'Julie'
♠ Q
♥ –
♦ 4
♣ J

Santhanee
♠ –
♥ Q
♦ Q J
♣ –

Chalalai
♠ J 10 9
♥ –
♦ –
♣ –

♠ A
♥ –
♦ 7 5
♣ –
Knight

Knight could scarcely believe the way the play had developed. He was going to make this contract! He led the jack of clubs, overruffing East's nine with the ace. Eleven tricks were before him and dummy's queen of trumps would provide a twelfth. The slam had been made.

Julie clapped her hands excitedly. 'We make slam,' she exclaimed. 'My Blackwood bids very good, yes?'

Knight gazed into her sparkling brown eyes. 'You bid it brilliantly,' he said.

'We change partners now,' said Santhanee, rising to her feet and trying to dislodge Julie from her chair.

'Mai chai!' declared Julie, pushing her back. 'I meet Rupert, not you. We stay partners.'

Knight could not believe his eyes. Two beautiful girls fighting over him? Whatever disasters might lie ahead of him during the remainder of the cruise, this afternoon in Pat Pong would more than make up for it.

The second rubber was soon under way. Santhanee went down unluckily in a couple of part-scores. Knight then arrived in a slam.

Love All   ♠ K J 5
Dealer South   ♥ 6
           ♦ K 7 4 3
           ♣ K J 10 9 6

West		East
♠ 9 8 4 2		♠ Q 10 7
♥ K 10 7 5 3 2	N W E S	♥ Q J 4
♦ 8		♦ Q J 10 6 2
♣ 7 4		♣ 8 3

           ♠ A 6 3
           ♥ A 9 8
           ♦ A 9 5
           ♣ A Q 5 2

WEST	NORTH	EAST	SOUTH
Santhanee	'Julie'	Chalalai	Rupert Knight
–	–	–	1♣
Pass	1♦	Pass	2NT
Pass	4♣	Pass	6♣
All Pass			

Santhanee led her singleton diamond and Julie mischievously refused to put down the dummy. 'You know how pleased you are when I holding four-card support?' she said.

'Yes,' said Knight.

'This time you very, very pleased,' continued Julie. 'I holding five-card trump support!'

'Excellent,' congratulated Knight. He surveyed the dummy closely, noting that the slam was a sound one. If diamonds were 3-3 or West held the spade queen, there would be an easy twelfth trick.

East played the 10 on the first round of diamonds and Knight won with the ace. He cashed the ace of hearts and ruffed a heart in dummy. A trump to the ace was followed by a second heart ruff. When Knight cashed the king of trumps, both defenders followed. He returned to his hand with the ace of spades, leaving this position:

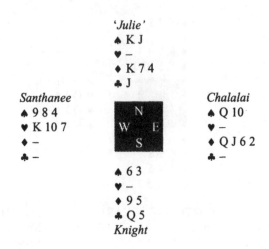

'*Julie*'
♠ K J
♥ —
♦ K 7 4
♣ J

Santhanee
♠ 9 8 4
♥ K 10 7
♦ —
♣ —

Chalalai
♠ Q 10
♥ —
♦ Q J 6 2
♣ —

♠ 6 3
♥ —
♦ 9 5
♣ Q 5
Knight

Pausing for a second, to gain the full attention of his attractive entourage, Knight now led ♦9. When West showed out, he ran the card and the girl from Chiang Rai won with the jack. Her eyes darted backwards and forwards, between her own hand and the dummy. 'Not like to lead to next trick,' she said.

Knight laughed and faced his remaining cards. 'If you play a spade or a diamond, dummy scores two tricks in the suit. If you have another heart to play, I can throw my spade loser and ruff in the dummy.'

Santhanee brought the score to Game All with a straightforward 3NT. A competitive auction arose on the next deal:

Game All   ♠ J 10 8 6 3
Dealer East   ♥ A 9 7 6 2
                    ♦ 10 8 4
                    ♣ —

♠ Q 7 5 2   ♠ 4
♥ —   N   ♥ K
♦ Q 9 6 2   W   E   ♦ A K 5 3
♣ A 9 7 6 3   S   ♣ K Q J 8 5 4 2

                    ♠ A K 9
                    ♥ Q J 10 8 5 4 3
                    ♦ J 7
                    ♣ 10

WEST	NORTH	EAST	SOUTH
Santhanee	'Julie'	Chalalai	Rupert Knight
–	–	1♣	1♥
1♠	4♥	5♣	5♥
6♣	6♥	Double	All Pass

The bidding ground to a halt in six hearts doubled and Santhanee led the ace of clubs. Knight ruffed in the dummy and played the ace of trumps.

'You look my hand!' cried Chalalai, as she reluctantly produced the king. 'Why you not take finesse?'

'Call me psychic,' replied an amused Knight. 'I had a strange feeling that the king would be singleton.'

West discarded a club on the first round of trumps. Knight then played a spade to the king, followed by a lead of the ♠9 from his hand.

Placing her partner with a doubleton ace of spades, Santhanee played low on the second round of spades. She emitted a loud squeal when her partner showed out on this trick. 'You tricking poor Santhanee!' she cried. 'How you know to play this way?'

Knight laughed. 'You did bid spades,' he replied.

The king of spades won the next trick and Knight crossed to dummy with a trump. A spade ruff set up a long card in the suit and he returned to dummy to throw one of his diamond losers on the long spade. The doubled slam had been made.

Julie ran round the table and threw her arms around Knight. 'You most wonderful bridge player!' she exclaimed. 'Me like you very, very much.'

Knight could not believe his luck. Back in England girls tended to judge solely by personal appearance. They would look the other way if, like him, you were unlucky enough to have lost most of your hair. Nor were they very impressed if you used your trouser belt as a stomach support. What a refreshing experience it was to be in the company of girls who could see past such physical shortcomings and appreciate an attractive personality.

Julie sat on Knight's lap and leaned forward to whisper in his ear. 'You, me, we go in back room together,' she said. 'I be your girlfriend.'

For one terrible moment Knight thought it must all be a dream. No, he could smell her jasmine scent and feel the weight of her slender frame on his knees. Paradise it might be but it was no dream. 'Yes, please,' he said.

Knight arrived back at the coach park with only five minutes to spare. He clambered up the steps and, somewhat out of breath, took a vacant seat next to Mark Rufus.

'You missed some fantastic temples,' Rufus informed him. 'One had a solid gold Bhuddha weighing over five tons. Did you have a good time yourself?'

Knight bore a dazed, slightly disbelieving, expression. 'The best time of my life,' he replied. 'Only one thing spoiled it slightly.'

'What's that?' Rufus enquired.

'When I came to pay the tuk-tuk driver who brought me back to the coach, I couldn't find my wallet,' said Knight. 'All my credit cards gone and two hundred US dollars. Must have dropped it some time during the day, I can't think how.'

'Wow!' exclaimed Rufus. 'You must have had a really good time if your day was only slightly spoiled.'

A smile came to Knight's lips, as the coach commenced its long journey back to the cruise ship. 'I did,' he replied.

3
Alice Vick's Fancy Play

'It's a special event tonight, ladies,' said Rupert Knight. 'We're holding a Random Teams. When all the pairs are here, I'll make a draw to determine everyone's team-mates.'

'I don't like the sound of that,' declared Ailsa Reid. 'What if we draw that pair who hesitated against us. You know, Rufus and Parker. They might think that we were letting them down.'

'I tell you what,' replied Knight. 'If you happen to draw Rufus and Parker, I'll put the card back and draw you someone else.'

'That's no good,' said Norma McBain. 'We might end up with some-one absolutely hopeless. There's no chance of winning if your other pair are beginners.'

'It's all part of the fun,' Knight persisted. 'You have to do your best, whoever your team-mates are.'

'It doesn't sound like fun to me,' declared Ailsa Reid. 'In fact, I'm not going to play.' She wagged an index finger in front of Knight's face. 'I'll expect a refund for the missed session, too. The cruise brochure never mentioned anything about Random Teams.'

'We're sorry to lose you, ladies,' called Knight, as the two Scotswomen beat their retreat.

Just for a change, Knight would be playing with a strong partner in this session. Mitzi Sucherman was having her hair tinted, so her hus-band Ralph had become available. The random draw presented them with Alice and Gordon Vick as team-mates. Could be worse, thought Knight, as he picked up these cards for the first board:

$$
\begin{array}{l}
\spadesuit \text{A K 7 5 4 3 2} \\
\heartsuit \text{8 3} \\
\diamondsuit \text{K 2} \\
\clubsuit \text{A 6}
\end{array}
$$

Ralph Sucherman opened 1♦ and he responded 1♠. Sucherman's 1NT rebid showed 15-17 points and Knight's thoughts now turned towards a slam. With at least two spades opposite, there was a fair chance of no trump losers. Surely he should be able to restrict the side-suit losers to one. 'Six Spades', said Knight.

This was the complete deal:

```
Love All                    ♠ 9
Dealer North                ♥ A K 5 2
                            ♦ A Q 8 7
                            ♣ K 5 4 2
        ♠ 8                               ♠ Q J 10 6
        ♥ J 10 9 4          N             ♥ Q 7 6
        ♦ J 9 6 5 4      W     E          ♦ 10 3
        ♣ Q 10 8            S             ♣ J 9 7 3
                            ♠ A K 7 5 4 3 2
                            ♥ 8 3
                            ♦ K 2
                            ♣ A 6
```

WEST	NORTH	EAST	SOUTH
Oakley	Ralph	Doris	Rupert
Hampton	Sucherman	Stokes	Knight
–	1♦	Pass	1♠
Pass	1NT	Pass	6♠
All Pass			

The jack of hearts was led and Sucherman put down three four-card suits, followed by a singleton trump. Knight raised an eyebrow. It was not his idea of good bidding to rebid 1NT with a singleton. Still, all his side suit losers were covered. The slam would be cold if trumps were 3-2. 'Win with the ace,' he said.

Doris Stokes, who suffered from rheumatism, always held her cards very low. Knight had no intention of looking at them but, before he could avert his eyes, he happened to notice that she held four trumps to the   Q-J-10. How unlucky! There was no chance of picking them up, was there? Was her small trump the eight or the six? Knight permitted his eyes to drift slightly to the right. Ah, her fourth trump was the six, leaving West with a singleton eight. 'Play the trump,' said Knight.

Doris Stokes covered with the 10. Knight won with the ace and - surprise, surprise - the eight fell on his left. Knight wondered about the ethics of the situation. He hadn't looked at East's hand deliberately. Not at first, anyway. Could he justify playing West for a singleton 8? Perhaps he could. East would hardly cover the 9 if she held Q-10-6 or J-10-6.

Knight crossed to the king of hearts and ruffed a heart, the queen appearing from East. He then cashed the ace and king of clubs and ruffed a club. Knight returned to dummy with the queen of diamonds and ruffed dummy's last club, East following suit. These cards remained:

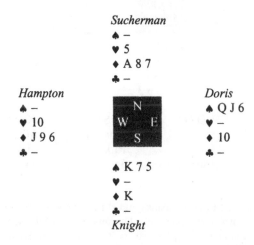

Sucherman
♠ –
♥ 5
♦ A 8 7
♣ –

Hampton
♠ –
♥ 10
♦ J 9 6
♣ –

Doris
♠ Q J 6
♥ –
♦ 10
♣ –

♠ K 7 5
♥ –
♦ K
♣ –
Knight

With victory in sight, Knight overtook the king of diamonds with the ace and called for the last heart. When Doris ruffed high, he under-ruffed with the five. She had to lead into his K-7 tenace and the slam was made.

Sucherman shook his head in amazed admiration. 'You played as if you could see through the backs of the cards!' he exclaimed. 'West's ♠8 could be from Q-J-8, J-8-6, Q-8, J-8 or 8-6. How you read it correctly, I have no idea.'

Knight assumed his most expert expression. 'Doris is a good player,' he replied. 'She wouldn't have covered unless she held Q-J-10-6.'

'From Q-J-10 bare she would not cover?' queried Sucherman.

'West would have no reason to play the eight in that case,' replied Knight. He turned in friendly fashion towards Oakley Hampton, who was sitting West. 'Unless it's one of your Golden Rules in Minnesota to play high-low from a doubleton trump.'

'Excellent result for us, anyway,' declared Sucherman. 'Our other pair will like this one!'

At that very moment Alice and Gordon Vick were, somewhat nervously, facing Rufus and Parker. The players had just drawn their cards for this deal:

North-South game
Dealer West

```
                    ♠ Q 7 4
                    ♥ K
                    ♦ A 6 5 4 2
                    ♣ Q J 10 5
    ♠ 9 8 3              N              ♠ 10 6 2
    ♥ A Q J 10 6                        ♥ 9 8 7 4 2
    ♦ J 10 9 7      W       E           ♦ Q 3
    ♣ A                  S              ♣ K 7 4
                    ♠ A K J 5
                    ♥ 5 3
                    ♦ K 8
                    ♣ 9 8 6 3 2
```

WEST	NORTH	EAST	SOUTH
Mark	Reverend	Jonathan	Alice
Rufus	Vick	Parker	Vick
1♥	Dble	3♥	4♠
All Pass			

Alice Vick arrived in Four Spades and Rufus led ♣A, hoping to be able to cross in hearts to receive a ruff. The appearance of the heart king in dummy put a stop to this plan. He switched to ♦J at Trick 2 and declarer won with dummy's ace.

With three top losers in the side suits, Mrs Vick needed to ruff a heart in dummy. 'King of hearts, please,' she said.

Rufus won with the heart ace and persisted with another diamond. Mrs Vick won with the king, ruffed a heart, and began to draw trumps. It was at this point that she noticed, to her horror, that the club suit was blocked. How careless! She must have followed with dummy's only low club spot-card on the first trick. Was there any way to recover?

On the third round of trumps, Mrs Vick discarded one of the blocking clubs from dummy. Trumps proved to be 3-3, she was pleased to see, and these cards remained:

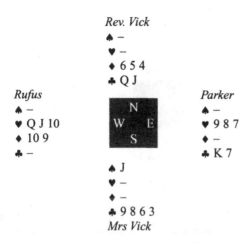

Rev. Vick
♠ —
♥ —
♦ 6 5 4
♣ Q J

Rufus
♠ —
♥ Q J 10
♦ 10 9
♣ —

Parker
♠ —
♥ 9 8 7
♦ —
♣ K 7

♠ J
♥ —
♦ —
♣ 9 8 6 3
Mrs Vick

Mrs Vick now played a club to the queen and king. A diamond return would have beaten the contract, forcing declarer's last trump and leaving the club suit blocked. Unfortunately for him, Parker had no diamond to play. When he returned a heart, declarer ruffed in her hand and threw dummy's last club away. 'These clubs are good, I think,' she said.

'Ah, well played, Alice!' congratulated the Reverend Vick. 'That was clever stuff in clubs. The suit was blocked, wasn't it?'

His wife nodded. 'I think I should have played one of your high clubs on the first round,' she said. 'Still, at least I made it.'

Rufus gave a small shake of the head as he entered the score in his card. 'A diamond lead works better,' he observed. 'I can play diamonds again when I get in with the two aces. That forces the South hand.'

'Or a trump lead, followed by a second trump when you win with the heart ace,' added Parker. 'If declarer takes her heart ruff, we can force her in hearts when she knocks out the clubs.'

'That's true,' replied Rufus. 'And if she plays on clubs instead I can play a third trump to stop the heart ruff.'

Alice Vick surveyed her opponents with a puzzled expression. How could they possibly remember the hand once it was over? It was all she could do to remember what the contract had been.

This was the next board:

East-West game
Dealer North

```
                    ♠ 6 2
                    ♥ A 7
                    ♦ A K 10 7 5 3
                    ♣ 9 8 2
     ♠ A 9 5                         ♠ 8 4
     ♥ K 9 8 4         N             ♥ Q J 5 2
     ♦ 9 6         W       E         ♦ Q J 2
     ♣ Q 10 5 4        S             ♣ A J 6 3
                    ♠ K Q J 10 7 3
                    ♥ 10 6 3
                    ♦ 8 4
                    ♣ K 7
```

WEST	NORTH	EAST	SOUTH
Mark	Reverend	Jonathan	Alice
Rufus	Vick	Parker	Vick
–	1♦	Pass	1♠
Pass	2♦	Pass	3♠
Pass	4♠	All Pass	

'Was your partner's 3♠ bid forcing?' enquired Mark Rufus, who was on lead.

'It was a jump bid, wasn't it?' Reverend Vick replied. 'That must be forcing. Alice would sign off in 2♠ with a weak hand.'

'I didn't mean it as forcing, actually,' said Mrs Vick.

'We'll be too high in that case,' declared Vick. 'I've only got eleven points.'

Rufus led ♣4 to his partner's ace. Alice Vick captured the club return with the king and paused to make a plan. What would happen if she played ace and another heart, preparing for a ruff? That was no good. They could stop the ruff by playing two rounds of trumps. If she then ducked a diamond, to set up the suit, they would have a second heart to cash.

What if she set up the diamonds straight away, cashing the ace-king and ruffing a third round high? That was no good either. When she played on trumps they would return a heart, killing the entry to dummy. And if she played on trumps straight away they would simply knock out the heart entry. It seemed there was no way to make it.

Suddenly Mrs Vick was struck by an amazing idea. What if she ducked the first round of hearts? If the defenders returned a second heart, she would be able to take a heart ruff. If instead they played on trumps, the ace of hearts would still be there as an eventual entry for the diamonds. Well, it worth a try, anyway.

Mrs Vick led a low heart from her hand and West produced the nine. 'Small, please, Gordon,' she said.

As declarer had foreseen, the defenders had no counter to this move. Parker overtook with the jack of hearts and returned a trump, West holding off the ace. Alice Vick cashed dummy's ace of hearts and returned to hand with a club ruff to trump her losing heart. Two rounds of diamonds stood up and she then ruffed a diamond high. She conceded a trick to the ace of trumps and the remaining tricks were hers.

'That was a fancy play in hearts, Alice,' said the Reverend Vick, looking uncertainly across the table. 'Did it make any difference?'

'Certainly did,' said Rufus. 'It was a clever effort.'

Alice Vick looked gratefully in Rufus's direction. It was nice of the young man to say so. Whether it was true or not.

Rufus looked across at his partner. 'That club return wasn't so hot,' he continued. 'Why didn't you play a trump?'

'Is that any good?' queried Parker. 'If you play two rounds of trumps, she can just draw trumps and set up the diamonds.'

'I duck the first round of trumps, of course,' replied Rufus. 'Try and make it then!'

Back on Knight's table, two fresh faces had arrived. Giles and Felicity Couttes-Browne, from Guildford in Surrey, had flown out to Bombay to join the world cruise. This would be Knight's first opportunity to assess their standard of play. They were certainly dressed very smartly. Look at the pearls she was wearing! If they were genuine, they must be worth a fortune.

'Ah, Giles and Felicity, good to see you,' said Knight. 'Are you enjoying your first session?'

Felicity Couttes-Browne peered down her considerable nose. 'I don't think much of the standard,' she replied. 'The lady at the next table couldn't even draw trumps. We took two ruffs each!'

'It's only meant to be for fun,' Knight replied. 'We don't take the game too seriously here.'

'That's very disappointing,' said Giles, a tall man with expensively-cut wavy hair. 'We only chose this cruise to get some good bridge in the evenings.'

'We do have a few strong players,' said Knight. 'It's my job to make sure everyone has an enjoyable time, whether they're good players or not.'

This was the first board of the round:

Love All
Dealer South

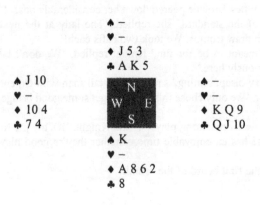

```
                    ♠ 4 3
                    ♥ A 7 6 4
                    ♦ J 5 3
                    ♣ A K 5 3
♠ Q J 10 9 7 6 5 2        N         ♠ 8
♥ 9                                 ♥ 5 2
♦ 10 4          W         E         ♦ K Q 9 7
♣ 7 4                    S          ♣ Q J 10 9 6 2
                    ♠ A K
                    ♥ K Q J 10 8 3
                    ♦ A 8 6 2
                    ♣ 8
```

WEST	NORTH	EAST	SOUTH
Felicity	Ralph	Giles	Rupert
C-Browne	Sucherman	C-Browne	Knight
–	–	–	1♥
4♠	5♥	Pass	6♥
All Pass			

Mrs Couttes-Browne led ♠Q and Knight won with the ace. There were eleven tricks on view but no clear route to a twelfth. East might well hold the sole guard of both minors, thought Knight. If he attempted to rectify the count by ducking a diamond, however, a club switch would kill a key entry to dummy.

Knight decided to run his winners in the majors immediately. It might then be possible to duck a trick after East had been squeezed. This position was soon reached:

```
                    ♠ –
                    ♥ –
                    ♦ J 5 3
                    ♣ A K 5
♠ J 10                   N          ♠ –
♥ –                                 ♥ –
♦ 10 4          W         E         ♦ K Q 9
♣ 7 4                    S          ♣ Q J 10
                    ♠ K
                    ♥ –
                    ♦ A 8 6 2
                    ♣ 8
```

Knight played the king of spades, throwing a diamond from dummy. Fairly sure that he held the only guard on dummy's club suit, Couttes-Browne threw ♦9.

Since there were still five clubs out, dummy's clubs couldn't possibly be good. Knight steeled himself to duck a diamond. If West had one of the top diamonds, she would win and cash a spade. So be it. There was nothing else he could try.

When a diamond was played to the jack, East won with the queen. Knight won the club return and cashed the dummy's other high club. His remaining diamonds proved to be good and the slam was made.

Knight was exultant. This hand had arrived at exactly the right moment, just when the snooty Surrey woman had been complaining about the poor standard.

Sucherman had taken no great liking to the new couple either. 'A club lead beats this,' he declared. 'A diamond lead too, I think. It breaks up the entry position.'

Felicity Couttes-Browne glared at Sucherman. What a rude man to criticise other people's play! She may have mentioned the lady at the other table playing poorly, but that was different. Everyone on a bridge cruise should be able to draw trumps, surely?

This was the next deal:

```
North-South game        ♠ 10 7 5 3 2
Dealer South            ♥ A K 10
                        ♦ 8 2
                        ♣ K 7 4
        ♠ 9                                 ♠ J 8 6 4
        ♥ 9 7 3 2           N               ♥ 8 6
        ♦ K 10 9 6 5 3  W       E           ♦ 7 4
        ♣ Q 8              S                 ♣ 10 9 6 5 2
                        ♠ A K Q
                        ♥ Q J 5 4
                        ♦ A Q J
                        ♣ A J 3
```

WEST	NORTH	EAST	SOUTH
Felicity	Ralph	Giles	Rupert
C-Browne	Sucherman	C-Browne	Knight
–	–	–	2♣
Pass	2♦	Pass	2NT
Pass	6NT	All Pass	

Recalling that her teacher back in Surrey had recommended seeking a safe lead against 6NT, Felicity Couttes-Browne led ♥2. 'I don't call that a negative response,' she observed, as the dummy went down. 'Do you, Giles? The man has an ace and two kings.'

For a short moment Ralph Sucherman narrowed his eyes. It was polite to refer to an opponent as 'the man', where they came from? What did she know about the game, anyway? On a hand such as his, it was best to keep the bidding low and hear partner's rebid. You could always show your strength later.

Knight won the heart lead with dummy's king and took an immediate diamond finesse. The queen lost to West's king and another heart was returned. Knight won in the dummy and tested the spade suit, discovering the 4-1 break. He continued to cash winners in the South hand, arriving at this position:

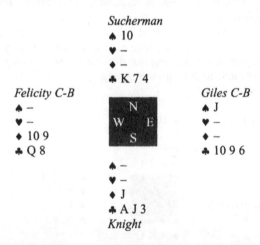

```
                    Sucherman
                    ♠ 10
                    ♥ –
                    ♦ –
                    ♣ K 7 4
   Felicity C-B                      Giles C-B
   ♠ –          ┌──────────┐         ♠ J
   ♥ –          │    N     │         ♥ –
   ♦ 10 9       │  W   E   │         ♦ –
   ♣ Q 8        │    S     │         ♣ 10 9 6
                └──────────┘
                    ♠ –
                    ♥ –
                    ♦ J
                    ♣ A J 3
                    Knight
```

Knight led ♦J, throwing a club from dummy. East, who had to retain his guard in spades, was forced to throw another club. Knight then crossed to the king of clubs and returned a second round of the suit towards his hand.

When ♣10 appeared from East, Knight knew how the cards lay. East's last card was the spade jack, so West must have started with the doubleton queen of clubs! He was determined to make the most of the situation. 'Oh dear,' he said. 'I hate it when a big hand comes down to a guess, right at the end.'

Felicity Couttes-Browne stared straight in front of her, determined not to give anything away.

Knight pulled one card from his hand, then replaced it and began to finger the other card. 'I don't know what to do,' he said eventually. 'I think I'll try the ace.'

With ill-disguised aggravation, Felicity Couttes-Browne contributed the queen to the trick. The slam had been made. 'That play was well against the odds,' she informed Knight. 'Giles started with five clubs and I had only two.'

'Yes, he was a 5-to-2 favourite to hold the queen,' Knight replied. 'Still, mathematics isn't everything. I had a feeling the queen would be doubleton.'

The evening's play was soon over and the Vicks returned to their home table to compare scores.

'We did quite well against Rufus and Parker,' said Mrs Vick excitedly. 'On one hand we actually had them arguing about how they should have defended.'

'Well done, indeed!' congratulated Knight.

'I went down in one game I should have made,' Mrs Vick continued, 'but we're quite good apart from that.'

A few minutes later, Knight collected the scores from the other teams then rose to his feet. 'First with a score of plus 83 IMPs were Alice and Gordon Vick, Ralph Sucherman and myself!' he said.

The Vicks waved victoriously while the other players applauded.

'Second, with a score of plus 59 IMPs were Doris Stokes, Oakley Hampton and...who was their other pair?' Knight paused to look at the team sheets. 'Ah yes, Rufus and Parker.'

'Third were one of our new pairs, the Couttes-Brownes, playing with Debbie and Sharon,' concluded Knight. 'A very good effort by the newcomers, who must have been nervous, playing their first game with us. A special round of applause for Felicity and Giles, please!'

4
Adventure in Haiphong Road

The *King Harald II* had docked for two nights in Hong Kong, allowing plenty of time to explore the delights of the former colony. On the first day the cruisers were taken to the covered Kowloon jade market. They then boarded the Star Ferry, from Kowloon to Hong Kong, and climbed to Victoria Peak on the funicular. A motorised longboat took them to a seafood lunch on a floating restaurant in Aberdeen. In the afternoon they boarded a tram to visit the Happy Valley racecourse, then returned to Kowloon to see the flower market, the bird market and finally the opening of the Temple Street night market. It was nearly eight o'clock when, tired but happy, they returned to the ship for dinner.

'That's enough sight-seeing for me,' declared Mark Rufus, as he donned his evening dress for the formal dinner that night. 'I'm looking for something different tomorrow.'

Parker checked his appearance in the mirror, adjusting his purple bow-tie. 'Anything in mind?' he asked.

'The Chinese are the greatest gambling nation in the world,' Rufus replied. 'I've been given an address where we might get some action. Haiphong Road - number 23, they said.'

'Is it safe, do you think?' asked Parker.

Rufus laughed. 'I wouldn't recommend it to Doris Stokes,' he replied. 'I think two lads like us can look after ourselves.'

The following afternoon Rufus and Parker made their way to Haiphong Road. There was an open doorway to number 23 and they climbed a narrow staircase. Several pairs of eyes turned their way as they entered a smoke-filled gaming room.

'You are lost?' asked an exceptionally overweight Chinaman.

'No,' replied Rufus. 'I was told there was a bridge game here.'

The Chinaman eyed them closely. 'You good players?' he said.

'Nothing special,' Rufus replied. 'More interested in the money aspect, really. We like gambling.'

The Chinaman nodded approvingly. 'You come to right place!' he exclaimed. 'Game in corner, 100 HK dollar stake. You play those two at partnership?'

Rufus peered into the far corner, where he could see two local play-

ers, one in short-sleeved white shirt, the other wearing oriental dress
and a black skull-cap.

'That'll be fine,' he said. 'What's the table money?'

'No charge for honourable visitors,' came the reply. 'You most welcome. C.K and Mr Hsu play for house.'

'How much is 100 Hong Kong dollars?' whispered Parker, as they
walked over to the far corner.

'About nine quid,' Rufus replied. 'Don't worry. I've got plenty of
money.'

The game was soon under way. Mr Hsu, who was elegantly attired in
a blue costume decorated with silver wire, was in his seventies. His
partner seemed to be in his mid-forties. This was an early deal:

```
Love All                  ♠ K Q 2
Dealer North              ♥ A 9 7 3
                          ♦ Q 5
                          ♣ A K 10 3
         ♠ -                              ♠ J 9 7 6
         ♥ K Q J 10 5 2     N            ♥ 4
         ♦ K 10 9 7      W     E          ♦ J 6 3
         ♣ 9 5 2            S             ♣ Q J 8 6 4
                          ♠ A 10 8 5 4 3
                          ♥ 8 6
                          ♦ A 8 4 2
                          ♣ 7
```

WEST	NORTH	EAST	SOUTH
Rufus	C.K.Chen	Parker	Mr Hsu
–	1♣	Pass	1♠
2♥	2NT	Pass	3♦
Pass	4♠	Pass	5♦
Pass	6♠	All Pass	

Rufus led ♥K, won in the dummy, and Mr Hsu cashed two clubs
immediately to dispose of his heart loser. To escape for one diamond
loser he would need to lead a diamond towards the queen, then ruff a
diamond. What was the best route to hand? It seemed obvious to ruff a
heart, but this might allow East to throw a diamond. If West went in
subsequently with the diamond king, he could play another top heart,
allowing a further diamond discard.

Mr Hsu preferred to ruff a club to his hand. When he next led a low diamond, West went in with the king. Declarer ruffed the queen of hearts continuation, East discarding a diamond. A diamond to dummy's queen left this position:

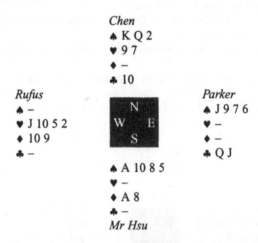

Chen
♠ K Q 2
♥ 9 7
♦ –
♣ 10

Rufus
♠ –
♥ J 10 5 2
♦ 10 9
♣ –

Parker
♠ J 9 7 6
♥ –
♦ –
♣ Q J

♠ A 10 8 5
♥ –
♦ A 8
♣ –
Mr Hsu

Mr Hsu leaned towards the dummy and played a heart. If Parker declined to ruff, declarer would continue with a cross-ruff, ruffing both diamonds high. With no great expectation that it would improve matters, Parker ruffed in with the seven. Declarer overruffed with the eight and ruffed a diamond with the king, East throwing a club.

When another heart was led, East had no winning option. If he ruffed in again, declarer would overruff and be able to draw trumps. The diamond ace would then be his twelfth trick. Parker decided to throw his last club instead. Declarer ruffed with the five, then ruffed the ace of diamonds with the queen. His last two cards were ♠A 10. With a complete count on the hand, Mr Hsu led a trump and calmly finessed the ten. It had been a long ride, over rough terrain, but the slam was home.

Rufus reached ruefully for his scorepad, beginning to wonder if they had stepped outside their league. Well stocked as his wallet might be, it would not survive too many big hands like that. Perhaps the cards would turn in their favour.

The wish was temporarily granted, Parker bringing the scores to Game All with an easy notrump game. Mr Hsu then had a chance to win the first rubber:

Game All   ♠ 3
Dealer West   ♥ 9
                 ♦ 10 8 5 4 3
                 ♣ K 10 9 6 5 2

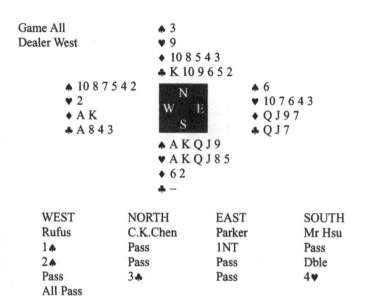

     ♠ 10 8 7 5 4 2   ♠ 6
     ♥ 2   ♥ 10 7 6 4 3
     ♦ A K   ♦ Q J 9 7
     ♣ A 8 4 3   ♣ Q J 7

                 ♠ A K Q J 9
                 ♥ A K Q J 8 5
                 ♦ 6 2
                 ♣ –

WEST	NORTH	EAST	SOUTH
Rufus	C.K.Chen	Parker	Mr Hsu
1♠	Pass	1NT	Pass
2♠	Pass	Pass	Dble
Pass	3♣	Pass	4♥
All Pass			

Mr Hsu passed 1NT on the first round, happy to take a bundle of
100s, should this prove to be the final contract. When the opener's
spade rebid ran back to him, he doubled - intending this to be for penal-
ties. Chen removed the double to 3♣ and Mr Hsu closed the auction
with a jump to game in hearts.

Rufus led the king of diamonds and continued with the ace. Not
wishing to damage his partner's trump holding, he refrained from a
trump switch. His next move was to place the ace of clubs on the table.
Mr Hsu ruffed with the five and cashed the ace of spades. The deal was
only four tricks old, but a rather unusual position had been reached:

C.K.Chen
♠ —
♥ 9
♦ 10 8 5
♣ K 10 9 6 5

Rufus
♠ 10 8 7 5 4
♥ 2
♦ —
♣ 8 4 3

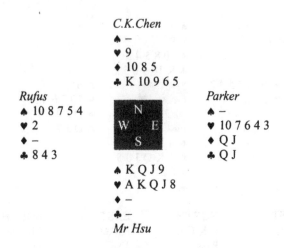

Parker
♠ —
♥ 10 7 6 4 3
♦ Q J
♣ Q J

♠ K Q J 9
♥ A K Q J 8
♦ —
♣ —

Mr Hsu

When Mr Hsu ruffed his ♠9 in the dummy, it was by no means obvious how Parker should defend in the East seat. If he overruffed, declarer would be able to ruff the minor-suit return, draw trumps, and claim the remainder. Since declarer would have to force himself, to return to hand, Parker preferred to keep his five-card trump holding intact. He eventually decided to throw a diamond.

Mr Hsu ruffed a diamond, removing East's last card in the suit and setting up two more winners in the dummy. He then drew four rounds of trumps. When he continued with the king of spades, Parker could see that it would be futile to ruff - he would have to concede the last two tricks to the dummy. He discarded a club instead, hoping that West held the spade queen. It was not to be. When Mr Hsu produced this card, East had to ruff and dummy's king of clubs claimed the last trick.

'I was squeezed in three suits, declared Parker. 'It's even worse if I throw a club. He plays the king, ten and nine of clubs through me. He makes an overtrick, then!'

The loss on the first rubber amounted to just over two hundred pounds each. For a brief moment, Rufus was tempted to abandon the game, avoiding any serious damage to their finances. One more rubber couldn't break the bank, though. Why shouldn't the cards turn in their favour?

Rufus was glad of his decision when he picked up a fair hand on the first deal of the new rubber. He was soon in a slam.

Love all
Dealer South

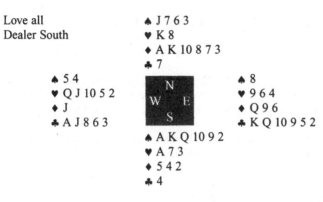

```
                    ♠ J 7 6 3
                    ♥ K 8
                    ♦ A K 10 8 7 3
                    ♣ 7
  ♠ 5 4                              ♠ 8
  ♥ Q J 10 5 2          N           ♥ 9 6 4
  ♦ J                W     E        ♦ Q 9 6
  ♣ A J 8 6 3           S           ♣ K Q 10 9 5 2
                    ♠ A K Q 10 9 2
                    ♥ A 7 3
                    ♦ 5 4 2
                    ♣ 4
```

WEST	NORTH	EAST	SOUTH
C.K.Chen	Parker	Mr Hsu	Rufus
–	–	–	1♠
Pass	2♦	Pass	3♠
Pass	4NT	Pass	5♣
Pass	6♠	All Pass	

Parker's 4NT was Roman Key-card Blackwood and the response showed either three aces or two aces and the king of trumps. The white-shirted Chinaman led ♥Q against the spade slam and down went the dummy. Rufus saw that everything would depend on bringing in the diamond suit for no losers.

What were the prospects in diamonds? If both defenders followed low on the first round, he would have to play for a 2-2 break. What if the ace dropped an honour from East on the first round? The Principle of Restricted Choice would apply. A finesse of dummy's 10 would be a 2-to-1 favourite, compared with playing to drop Q-J doubleton.

Rufus won the heart lead with the king and drew trumps in two rounds. When he played a diamond to the ace, the jack appeared from West. This was not what he had been hoping to see. If the jack was a singleton, there would be no way to make the contract. Suddenly two wires inside Rufus's brain made contact. Of course! He could eliminate the hearts, then exit in clubs. That would allow him to make the slam even if West's ♦J was a singleton.

Rufus cashed the king and ace of hearts and ruffed a heart. When he exited with a club, the defenders were left without resource. If West won, he would have to give a ruff-and-discard. In fact Mr Hsu, sitting East, won the club exit with the king. Unwilling to lead into dummy's diamond tenace, he returned a second club. Rufus threw his diamond loser from hand and ruffed in the dummy. The remaining tricks were his.

'Wo syu yàu jyàu yi wèi yi sheng!' cried Mr Hsu. 'Jèi shi yin yòng shwei ma!'

Chen shrunk to the back of his chair, his eyes resembling those of a frightened rabbit. It was clear to Rufus and Parker that he was being reprimanded for not leading the ace of clubs at Trick 1. This would have prevented the endplay.

Rufus could not believe his luck when, on the very next deal, he had a chance to capture the second rubber.

North-South game
Dealer West

```
                    ♠ 7
                    ♥ J 7 6 4
                    ♦ K Q 10 6 4
                    ♣ A K 2
  ♠ K Q J 9 8 3              ♠ 5 4 2
  ♥ –              N         ♥ Q 10 9 8 2
  ♦ A 5        W     E       ♦ 9 3 2
  ♣ J 9 8 6 3      S         ♣ Q 10
                    ♠ A 10 6
                    ♥ A K 5 3
                    ♦ J 8 7
                    ♣ 7 5 4
```

WEST	NORTH	EAST	SOUTH
C.K.Chen	Parker	Mr Hsu	Rufus
1♠	Dble	Pass	3♥
3♠	4♥	Dble	All Pass

Rufus won the spade king lead with the ace and cashed the ace of trumps, discovering the 5-0 break. To think that a few moments ago he had been thinking how lucky he was! There was a certain loser in diamonds, as well as three apparent losers in the trump suit. It seemed that he would have to throw his club loser on the diamonds, to escape for one down.

At Trick 3 Rufus led a diamond to the king. Hoping that it was West who held the doubleton diamond, he continued with the queen of diamonds. Chen won with the ace and switched to a club, won in the dummy. Rufus crossed to hand with the carefully preserved diamond jack, East following suit, then ruffed a spade in dummy. He cashed dummy's remaining club honour and surveyed this end position:

Parker
- ♠ —
- ♥ J 7
- ♦ 10 6
- ♣ 2

C.K.Chen
- ♠ Q J
- ♥ —
- ♦ —
- ♣ J 9 8

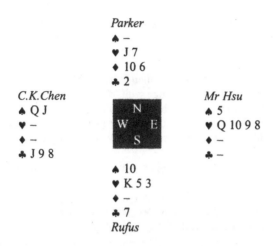

Mr Hsu
- ♠ 5
- ♥ Q 10 9 8
- ♦ —
- ♣ —

- ♠ 10
- ♥ K 5 3
- ♦ —
- ♣ 7

Rufus

Rufus now played one of dummy's established diamonds. Mr Hsu, sitting East, could not afford to let the diamond score a trick. He ruffed with the eight and Rufus paused to calculate his discard. East had played his spot-cards upwards on the first two rounds of spades. It therefore seemed that his four remaining trumps were accompanied by a spade. If a club was thrown on this trick, East would exit with a spade, forcing the dummy's ♥7. With the jack of trumps then bare, it would not be possible to deprive East of two further trump tricks.

Trying something different, Rufus threw ♠10 from hand. The ancient Chinaman could anticipate his fate if he exited with the ten or nine of trumps. Declarer would run it to the jack and lead the other master diamond, throwing his club loser as East ruffed with his penultimate trump. South's K-5 of trumps would then be good for the last two tricks. Nor would an exit with the trump queen be productive. Declarer would win with the king, cross to the jack of trumps, and lead another diamond to score his last trump en passant.

Mr Hsu eventually exited with ♠5, Rufus ruffing in his hand and throwing a diamond from dummy. When he then led a club, East had to ruff his partner's club winner and lead away from the queen of trumps. Ten tricks had been made.

'Great play, Mark!' Parker exclaimed.

Mr Hsu reached for his wallet and counted out a large bundle of Hong Kong dollars. He then beckoned to the gigantic owner of the establishment, hissing some request in Mandarin. The man soon returned with two hand-rolled reefers, about twice the width of a normal cigarette.

Rufus and Parker exchanged a glance. Wow! They looked as if they would pack quite a punch.

Chen leaned forward. 'You would like to join us for a smoke, while we play third rubber?' he enquired.

Parker was tempted. 'What's in them?' he asked.

Chen conducted a brief exchange with Mr Hsu in Mandarin. 'He say black weed from Laos. Not the best, but quite good.'

Parker looked across at Rufus. 'Shall we give it a try?' he said.

Rufus nodded and two more reefers, as well packed as the first two, were brought to the table.

'You like it?' asked Chen, laughing at Parker's reaction to his first drag.

Parker was finding it difficult not to cough. 'Yeah, it's good,' he spluttered. 'Stronger than the stuff we get back home.'

This was the opening deal of the third rubber:

```
Love all                  ♠ A 7 6 5 3
Dealer South              ♥ —
                          ♦ 9 6 4 2
                          ♣ A K 3 2
        ♠ K Q                              ♠ J 10 4
        ♥ J 9 8            N                ♥ 10 7 6 4 3
        ♦ Q J 3         W     E             ♦ 10 8
        ♣ J 9 6 5 4        S                ♣ Q 10 8
                          ♠ 9 8 2
                          ♥ A K Q 5 2
                          ♦ A K 7 5
                          ♣ 7
```

WEST	NORTH	EAST	SOUTH
Rufus	C.K.Chen	Parker	Mr Hsu
–	–	–	1♥
Pass	1♠	Pass	2♦
Pass	4♦	Pass	4NT
Pass	5♥	Pass	6♦
All Pass			

Rufus winced as the elderly Chinaman reached yet another big contract. He led the king of spades against the diamond slam and Mr Hsu won with dummy's ace.

The slam was a poor one. The trumps would have to break 3-2, obviously. It seemed he would also need hearts to be 4-4. It would then be possible draw two rounds of trumps, ruff the hearts good, and throw four of dummy's spades on the hearts. A cross-ruff would then produce twelve tricks

Maintaining his implacable expression, Mr Hsu drew two rounds of trumps. He then played three rounds of hearts, throwing two spades from the table. When a fourth round of hearts was led, West could not afford to ruff or declarer would throw dummy's last spade. He discarded a club and the trick was ruffed in dummy. Mr Hsu continued with two top clubs and a club ruff in his hand. This end position had been reached:

C.K.Chen
♠ 7
♥ —
♦ 9
♣ 3

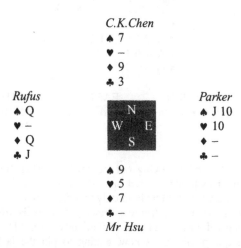

Rufus
♠ Q
♥ —
♦ Q
♣ J

Parker
♠ J 10
♥ 10
♦ —
♣ —

♠ 9
♥ 5
♦ 7
♣ —

Mr Hsu

Declarer now led his last heart. If West ruffed with his master trump, declarer would throw a spade from dummy and score the last two tricks on a crossruff. If instead West threw ♣J, dummy would ruff and West would then have to ruff the established ♣3. Declarer's last trump would be good for a twelfth trick.

Rufus was becoming quite light-headed from the effects of the reefer. Pleasant as the sensation might be, it was no great advantage when defending a slam at such high stakes. He eventually decided to throw ♠Q.

Mr Hsu ruffed in the dummy and now scored his last trump by ruffing a club. West had to follow suit and the slam was home.

Rufus drew deeply on his reefer, then thought back over the hand. Wow! Had that been a great hand or did it just look good after a few puffs of this strong black stuff?

The Englishmen exchanged a glance. Could they have done anything about it? It seemed not. The game continued, Rufus going down in a part-score and a game. Mr Hsu then had a chance to land the third rubber.

```
North-South game          ♠ K Q 7 4 2
Dealer East               ♥ 5
                          ♦ 9 7 3
                          ♣ J 9 6 5

      ♠ 9 8 5                            ♠ A J 10 6 3
      ♥ J 8 2          N                 ♥ K 6
      ♦ Q J 8 5     W     E              ♦ 10 2
      ♣ 7 4 2          S                 ♣ A K 8 3

                          ♠ –
                          ♥ A Q 10 9 7 4 3
                          ♦ A K 6 4
                          ♣ Q 10
```

WEST	NORTH	EAST	SOUTH
Rufus	C.K.Chen	Parker	Mr Hsu
–	–	1♠	4♥
All Pass			

Rufus led ♠9, covered by the king and ace. Mr Hsu ruffed, then drew deeply on his reefer as he considered his prospects. The only chance was an endplay on East, should he hold only two diamonds.

Mr Hsu cashed the ace of trumps, drawing low cards from the defenders, then cashed the ace and king of diamonds. It would be pointless to play the queen of trumps now, aiming to pin the jack. The defender who won with the king would then have an easy exit in trumps. Instead, Mr Hsu led a low trump.

Parker won with the bare king and, just as declarer had hoped, he had no diamond to play. He marked time by cashing the king of clubs. Declarer contributed the queen and Rufus signalled his count with the two. Ace and another club would put declarer in dummy and allow two discards - one on ♠Q, one on ♣J. It therefore seemed better to concede only one trick by exiting with the spade jack.

Mr Hsu nodded to himself when he saw this card. If he discarded one of his losers, winning with dummy's ♠Q, he would still go one down. East would have a safe spade exit when he was thrown in again with a club. Instead, Mr Hsu ruffed the spade exit. He drew West's outstanding trump, then led ♣10, overtaking with dummy's jack. It was the end of the road for Parker in the East seat. If he ducked, declarer would throw a diamond on the spade queen and claim ten tricks. Parker won the club trick but, with only black cards in his hand, he had to return the lead to dummy. Away went South's two diamond losers and the contract had been made.

Mr Hsu chuckled to himself and muttered a few words of Mandarin to his partner. C.K.Chen laughed back

Rufus took a consoling draw on his joint, then reached for his wallet. 'What's so amusing?' he asked.

'Mr Hsu say you can beat it,' Chen replied. 'If Johnnie hold back spade ace at Trick 1, he not get endplayed later. Declarer throw one loser but when Johnnie take trump king he can win two clubs and play spade ace.'

'My name's Jonathan, actually,' replied Parker sourly. 'Holding up the spade ace would be a completely mad thing to do.'

A further large bundle of Hong Kong dollars changed hands. 'Shall we give them one more rubber?' said Rufus, looking across the table in somewhat bleary-eyed fashion.

Parker was cautious by nature and would normally have called a halt at this stage. The joint had induced such a feeling of well-being, however, that he could barely conceive they would lose the next rubber. 'Yeah, go on,' he replied.

```
Love all              ♠ A K 6 3
Dealer North          ♥ Q J 3
                      ♦ 9 7 4
                      ♣ K 8 6
        ♠ 8 4              N           ♠ J 7 2
        ♥ A K 6 5      W       E       ♥ 9 7 2
        ♦ K 10 8 3                     ♦ J 6 5
        ♣ J 4 3            S           ♣ 9 7 5 2
                      ♠ Q 10 9 5
                      ♥ 10 8 4
                      ♦ A Q 2
                      ♣ A Q 10
```

WEST	NORTH	EAST	SOUTH
Rufus	C.K.Chen	Parker	Mr Hsu
–	1♣	Pass	1♠
Pass	2♠	Pass	4♠
All Pass			

Mark Rufus led ♥A against the spade game. Although Parker would normally signal attitude on an ace lead, there was no point when the queen was in the dummy. He followed with the two, showing an odd number of hearts. Not wishing to open a new suit, Rufus continued with king and another heart, dummy winning the third round.

Mr Hsu drew trumps and continued with three rounds of clubs, leaving the dummy on lead. After a brief pause he leaned forward and led ♦7. Parker, who was aware of the elimination situation, eventually covered with the jack. Declarer put on the queen, losing to West's king. A fourth round of hearts would give a ruff-and-discard, so Rufus had to return a diamond. Mr Hsu put up dummy's ♦9 and the game was made.

'Good play, that seven of diamonds,' observed Rufus, who was beginning to slur his speech. 'Running the nine works when I hold K-J-10. Running the seven works against K-J-8 or K-10-8.'

'Dwei bu chi,' declared Mr Hsu. 'Tse swô dzai náli hwai ywan.'

'Mr Hsu say our bidding not the best,' Chen explained to the Englishmen. 'Hand play better in no-trumps.'

Parker leaned towards the white-shirted Chinaman, ending a few inches from his face. 'Tell him he played it pretty well in spades,' he said.

Two failing contracts later, Mr Hsu arrived in a slam that could cost the Englishmen a considerable sum. This was the deal:

North-South game   ♠ A K Q 10 6 5
Dealer West   ♥ K 9 5
  ♦ 9 3
  ♣ K Q

♠ 8		♠ 7 4 3
♥ J 10	N	♥ Q 8 4 2
♦ A Q J 10 7 4 2	W E	♦ 8 6
♣ 9 4 2	S	♣ J 10 7 3

  ♠ J 9 2
  ♥ A 7 6 3
  ♦ K 5
  ♣ A 8 6 5

WEST	NORTH	EAST	SOUTH
Rufus	C.K.Chen	Parker	Mr Hsu
3♦	4♠	Pass	4NT
Pass	5♦	Pass	6NT
All Pass			

Rufus led ♥J and Mr Hsu inspected the dummy with no great enthusiasm. He won the first trick with the heart king and, with nothing better to do, ran dummy's spades. Parker threw one heart and one diamond, but was under mounting pressure in this end position:

C.K.Chen
♠ 5
♥ 9 5
♦ 9 3
♣ K Q

Rufus
♠ –
♥ 10
♦ A Q J
♣ 9 4 2

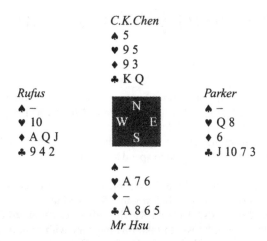

Parker
♠ –
♥ Q 8
♦ 6
♣ J 10 7 3

♠ –
♥ A 7 6
♦ –
♣ A 8 6 5
Mr Hsu

On the last spade Parker had to throw a diamond, abandoning the link with his partner's hand. Since no clubs had been thrown, Mr Hsu knew that his fourth club was not good. He discarded ♣5 from his hand and proceeded to cash the two top clubs in dummy. Ace and another heart then threw East on lead. He had to return a club and declarer faced his last two clubs, the club ace and a good heart. The slam had been made.

Rufus surveyed his partner through heavy-lidded eyes. 'Nothing we could do, was there?' he asked.

'Don't think so,' came the reply. 'I can't really think straight at the moment. My God, this stuff is strong!'

C.K.Chen, seemingly unaffected by the fact that he was already on his third reefer, turned to the score-sheet. 'Four thousand two hundred HK dollar,' he informed his opponents. He bared his teeth in a wide grin. 'We throw in the joint for no charge.'

Rufus paid for the rubber, noting that his wallet was almost empty. 'Tell him we enjoyed the game,' he declared, rising unsteadily to his feet.

Chen nodded and rattled off a few words of Mandarin.

Mr Hsu was finding some difficulty accommodating the winnings in his wallet. Rufus could not believe what he saw. The guy must have a couple of thousand quid in there!

'M goi fung shui,' said Mr Hsu. 'Tcheng pak pai Kow-lun gwaio yam.'

'Next time in Hong Kong you most welcome here,' Chen translated.

'Very kind of him,' said Mark Rufus. 'If I ever feel the need for a five hundred pound reefer again, I'll know where to come!'

5
The Distinguished Visitor

Rupert Knight could not contain his excitement. The world famous Martin Hoffman had boarded the *King Harald II* and had been persuaded to play one session of duplicate.

Knight basked in the reflected glory as he and Hoffman entered the card-room together. 'We'll need to spend some time discussing our system,' he said.

'No, no, keep it simple,' Hoffman replied. 'Strong notrump. Weak two in three suits. All doubles below game for take-out.'

'Very sound methods,' declared Knight. Whatever happened during the rest of the cruise, he would take this memory with him. A whole session in partnership with the great Hoffman. 'Take your seats, everyone!' he called.

Doris Stokes approached, leaning heavily on her walking stick. 'I don't have a partner tonight,' she said. 'I was going to play with Myrtle, but that singer she likes is on the cabaret.'

'I don't have a partner either, I'm afraid,' said the 30-year-old Mark Rufus, arriving on the scene.

Knight breathed a sigh of relief. 'That's fine, then,' he said. 'You and Doris can play together.'

Doris looked shell-shocked. 'No, no, he's *much* too good,' she declared. 'I get nervous if I play with a good partner. Why can't I play with you? Mark can play with er... this man.'

Knight's world was collapsing. Surely he wouldn't be robbed of such a glorious opportunity. He could have spent the rest of his life saying 'A similar hand came up when I was partnering Martin Hoffman.' His spirits sank as he saw Hoffman and Rufus walking towards a vacant East-West position.

'That's better,' said Doris, as she and Knight sat down at Table 1. 'I so enjoyed it last time we played together.'

The first few rounds ticked by with a predictable mixture of good and bad boards. Knight gathered his concentration as he saw Hoffman and Rufus approaching the table. With any luck he would have an interesting hand to play. 'And there was absolutely nothing Hoffman could do,' he would be able to say.

Hoffman and Rufus took their seats and this was the first board:

```
Love All              ♠ J 6 4
Dealer East           ♥ 7 4 2
                      ♦ A 10 8 6
                      ♣ 10 9 2

   ♠ Q 9 7 5            N            ♠ K 8 2
   ♥ Q 10 8 6 5                      ♥ J 9
   ♦ 7 5          W         E        ♦ K 9 3 2
   ♣ A 7               S            ♣ 8 6 5 4

                      ♠ A 10 3
                      ♥ A K 3
                      ♦ Q J 4
                      ♣ K Q J 3
```

WEST	NORTH	EAST	SOUTH
Martin	Doris	Mark	Rupert
Hoffman	Stokes	Rufus	Knight
–	–	Pass	2NT
Pass	3NT	All Pass	

Hoffman led ♥6 against 3NT and Knight studied the dummy carefully. If the diamond finesse was wrong, he would have to lose the lead twice in order to establish nine tricks. It therefore seemed a good idea to hold up in hearts, aiming to break the defenders' communications.

East's ♥J took the first trick and Knight won the heart continuation. When the king of clubs was played, Hoffman took his ace immediately. Clearing the heart suit would have been unproductive, since the diamond finesse was into the safe hand. Hoffman tried his luck with a spade switch instead, hoping to find his partner with such as K-10-x in the suit. It was not to be. Declarer's spades could withstand this attack and by playing on diamonds he brought his total to nine tricks.

'Well played indeed, Rupert!' said Doris Stokes.

Knight turned towards Hoffman, hoping to receive a small compliment for his hold-up with two stoppers.

'The way it went, we might beat this one,' Hoffman informed his partner. 'If you switch to a low spade at Trick 2, he ducks, wins the next spade and must guess which minor to play. If he plays on diamonds first, placing you with the long spade, he goes down.'

Doris had never heard anyone speak so quickly. She wouldn't have understood a word of it anyway, no doubt, but that was no excuse for such a lack of consideration.

Hoffman smiled to himself. 'Even better, in fact, if you switch to the king of spades!' he said. 'That beats it for sure. Declarer cannot duck or we make three spade tricks. If he takes the ace and clears the clubs, I play a low spade to keep communications.'

Knight nodded learnedly. 'That's the defence I was worried about,' he said.

'You can prevent it,' said Hoffman. 'Win the first heart, then play on clubs, attacking the entry to the danger hand.'

Doris had endured enough of this incomprehensible post mortem. She tapped a finger on her watch, indicating that time was running on.

East-West game
Dealer South

	♠ 8	
	♥ Q J 10 4 2	
	♦ A K 8 3	
	♣ 7 6 4	
♠ Q 6 5 4		♠ K 10 7 3 2
♥ 7 5 3	N	♥ 8
♦ 9 2	W E	♦ J 10 7 5
♣ K J 8 5	S	♣ 10 9 2
	♠ A J 9	
	♥ A K 9 6	
	♦ Q 6 4	
	♣ A Q 3	

WEST	NORTH	EAST	SOUTH
Martin	Doris	Mark	Rupert
Hoffman	Stokes	Rufus	Knight
–	–	–	2NT
Pass	3♦	Pass	3♥
Pass	4♦	Pass	4♥
Pass	6♥	All Pass	

Hoffman led a trump against the small slam in hearts and Doris Stokes laid out the dummy. 'Twelve points for you, including two for the singleton,' she said. 'That should be enough, facing a 2NT opening.'

Knight won the trump lead and drew trumps in two further rounds, East throwing a spade and a club. Three rounds of diamonds revealed the 4-2 break. What next?

It seemed to Knight that there was no need to take a club finesse immediately. He could play a spade to the nine first. If this drew an honour, West would be endplayed, forced to lead into one of the black-suit tenaces. If the ♠9 lost to the 10, nothing would be lost. Even if West found the best return of a spade, he could still fall back on the club finesse.

When Knight called for a spade, East contributed the three. Declarer's nine forced the queen from Hoffman and Knight then faced his remaining cards. 'You have to play into one of my black suits,' he said.

Hoffman nodded and returned his cards to the wallet. 'You can stop this by rising with the king of spades,' he informed his partner. 'Declarer can still make it, of course. He wins the ace, ruffs the spade nine, and ruffs the last diamond. I am down to queen-one spade, king-jack-one club. If I throw a spade, I'm endplayed with the queen; if I throw a club, he ducks a club. Still, that's more difficult for him. He may go wrong.'

Doris's head was spinning. How was it possible for anyone to speak so quickly? She glared disapprovingly at Hoffman, then reached into her handbag for a headache pill. The sooner this round was over, the better.

This was the next board:

East-West game	♠ A Q J 8 6 5	
Dealer West	♥ 9 6 2	
	♦ 5	
	♣ Q 3 2	

♠ 9 7		♠ 4 2
♥ Q J 10 8 7 3		♥ 5
♦ A 9 6		♦ Q J 10 7 4 3
♣ 10 4		♣ J 9 8 6

	♠ K 10 3	
	♥ A K 4	
	♦ K 8 2	
	♣ A K 7 5	

WEST	NORTH	EAST	SOUTH
Martin	Doris	Mark	Rupert
Hoffman	Stokes	Rufus	Knight
2♥	Pass	Pass	2NT
Pass	3♥	Pass	4♠
Pass	5♠	Pass	6♠
All Pass			

Hoffman opened with a weak two and an uncertain transfer auction carried Rupert Knight to a spade slam. The queen of hearts was led and down went the dummy.

'Not many points for you, I'm afraid,' said Doris Stokes, 'but I do have a nice six-timer in spades.'

Knight counted the top tricks on display. Eleven for sure, twelve if the clubs broke 3-3. Prospects of the ace of diamonds being onside were poor, after West's vulnerable weak two. 'Nice hand, Doris,' he said. 'Small, please.'

Knight won the opening lead with the ace of hearts and drew trumps in two rounds. He tested the club suit but no luck came. West showed out on the third round and Knight proceeded to ruff the fourth round. When two more rounds of trumps were played, Hoffman had to retain two hearts and was therefore forced to reduce the protection on his diamond ace. This was the position:

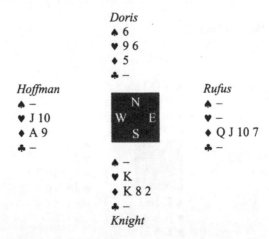

Doris
♠ 6
♥ 9 6
♦ 5
♣ —

Hoffman
♠ —
♥ J 10
♦ A 9
♣ —

Rufus
♠ —
♥ —
♦ Q J 10 7
♣ —

Knight
♠ —
♥ K
♦ K 8 2
♣ —

Knight led a diamond from dummy and Rufus went up with the queen. The moment of truth had arrived. Surely East could not hold the ace of diamonds. That would leave Hoffman with little more than a three-count for his vulnerable opening. Knight contributed the two from his hand and Hoffman followed with the nine. When Rufus continued with the jack of diamonds, Knight again played low. The ace appeared from Hoffman and the slam had been made.

Knight was exultant. Yes! He had played the hand brilliantly, facing the great Hoffman.

'He should not make this,' muttered Hoffman. 'Difficult for you, I realise, but you must play the seven on the first round of diamonds. I win with the nine and can exit with a heart.'

It gets better and better, thought Knight. Not only had he performed like a superstar himself, Rufus had apparently butchered the defence.

'The queen can never gain, do you see?' continued Hoffman. 'If declarer has king-nine, he will always make it.'

Mark Rufus scratched his cheek. 'I suppose so,' he replied. 'Playing the seven would never occur to me in a million years.'

Since a six-table Mitchell was in play, there were four boards in each round. Knight could scarcely believe it when, yet again, he ended at the helm. What was more, the contract was a grand slam.

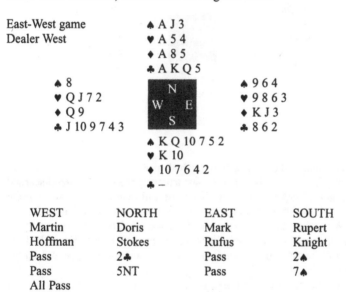

East-West game
Dealer West

North: ♠ A J 3 ♥ A 5 4 ♦ A 8 5 ♣ A K Q 5

West: ♠ 8 ♥ Q J 7 2 ♦ Q 9 ♣ J 10 9 7 4 3

East: ♠ 9 6 4 ♥ 9 8 6 3 ♦ K J 3 ♣ 8 6 2

South: ♠ K Q 10 7 5 2 ♥ K 10 ♦ 10 7 6 4 2 ♣ —

WEST	NORTH	EAST	SOUTH
Martin	Doris	Mark	Rupert
Hoffman	Stokes	Rufus	Knight
Pass	2♣	Pass	2♠
Pass	5NT	Pass	7♠
All Pass			

Hoffman led the jack of clubs and Knight won with dummy's ace, throwing a diamond. What was Doris thinking of, heading straight for a grand slam? She barely had a 2♣ opening in the first place. Playing against someone so famous must have gone to her head; she had overbid on nearly every board.

Knight cashed the ace and jack of spades, finding that East still held a trump. Was there any chance of a make? What if West had the sole guard on clubs and a singleton diamond, leaving East to guard the diamond suit? There would then be a double squeeze around the hearts.

Wow! That would impress the great man.

To simplify the position, Knight decided to cash dummy's remaining club honours before running the trumps. East had signalled count with the ♣2 on the first round, so there was not much risk attached to this. The king and queen of clubs duly stood up and Knight ran his remaining trumps. This end position arose:

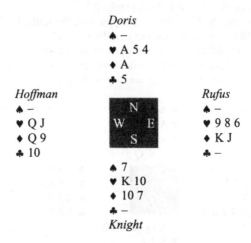

Doris
♠ –
♥ A 5 4
♦ A
♣ 5

Hoffman
♠ –
♥ Q J
♦ Q 9
♣ 10

Rufus
♠ –
♥ 9 8 6
♦ K J
♣ –

♠ 7
♥ K 10
♦ 10 7
♣ –
Knight

Hoffman, who until this point had made all his plays at lightning speed, paused briefly when the last trump appeared. He then discarded the jack of hearts. Knowing that West still held a club guard, Knight threw the ♣5 from dummy. Rufus discarded the jack of diamonds.

With three diamonds still out, there was no future in crossing to the ace of diamonds. The only hope was to play on hearts. He cashed the king of hearts and - miracle of miracles - the queen appeared on his left!

'I make it now,' exclaimed Knight. 'The ten of hearts is good and I can cross in diamonds to make the ace of hearts.'

'You played it well,' congratulated Hoffman. 'If I keep three hearts and a club, partner has to guard the diamonds. You cross to the diamond ace, return to the heart king, then play the last trump. There's a double squeeze around hearts.'

Knight, who had no clear idea of how he had managed to make the contract, was determined to make the most of the moment. 'That's what I had in mind,' he said.

Hoffman smiled as a thought occurred to him. 'I can beat this one, do you see how? If I lead diamond nine at Trick 1, this knocks out the ace and I retain a guard in the suit. You can't make it then.'

Doris reached once more for her headache pills. If this silly man carried on talking so fast, her head would never survive the experience.

'Even heart queen lead is good enough, I think,' continued Hoffman. 'Yes, with the heart king removed, we can both throw diamonds. You see what happens? The diamond ace blocks the suit.'

'Blocks the suit, yes,' said Knight. 'Still, don't blame yourself for the lead, Martin. Holding your cards, even I would have led a club!'

6
Temple of the Breeze

The *King Harald II* had docked for two full days in the impressive harbour of Osaka, in the Southern part of Japan. Mark Rufus had been given an introductory letter to a local celebrity, a Shinto priest who had studied bridge for over half a century. Rufus, Parker and Rupert Knight were very much looking forward to meeting the old man, who regarded the game as the finest mental discipline the world had to offer.

'I didn't realise it would be this far,' Knight declared, leaning forward from the back seat of the taxi. 'Have you seen the meter? It's over 9,000 yen already.'

'That's all right when we're dividing by three,' Rufus replied.

After a full hour's drive, ending in a steep climb, the taxi pulled into the forecourt of the Temple of the Breeze. Knight settled up for the taxi and the three walked past some weeping willows to the main building, built of pale stone.

'The driver didn't seem very pleased,' Parker observed. 'Did you give him a tip?'

'You must be joking,' Knight replied. 'He charged us a week's wages for a one-hour drive, as it was.'

The four were admitted to the temple by the resident gatekeeper, a middle-aged man in a plain black robe.

'We're here to meet Ikonishi-san,' Rufus informed him.

'He awaits your visit with much pleasure,' the gatekeeper replied.

'Perhaps you can tell us,' said Knight. 'Does he speak English.'

The gatekeeper laughed. 'Ikonishi-san is fluent in twenty-seven languages,' he replied. 'Last year he taught himself Albanian, a vocabulary of over seven thousand words, but - most bad luck - he has not had the chance to practise it yet. Do any of you speak Albanian?'

Rufus surveyed his colleagues quizzically. 'No, I'm afraid not,' he replied.

The three Englishmen were escorted to a walled garden, lined with almond trees, where the elderly Ikonishi was already seated at a card table. Also clad in a plain, black robe, he rose to his feet and administered a small bow. 'I have looked forward most heartily to your visit,' he declared. He pointed a finger at Knight. 'I will partner you for the first rubber, I think. I am not superstitious, by nature, but bald people have always brought me good luck!'

Knight surveyed the ancient priest somewhat curiously. 'Do you like to play for a stake?' he enquired.

Ikonishi closed his eyes, as if in pain. 'Such a beautiful game,' he replied. 'Should one taint it with capitalist desires?'

'No, no, I quite agree,' said Knight. He performed a quick shuffle of the cards and passed them across the table for the priest to cut.

With a serene smile, Ikonishiki pushed the deck towards the dealer. 'A cut of the cards is not necessary unless you distrust the shuffler,' he explained. 'Let me apologise in advance for the modest standard of my own play.'

Mark Rufus proceeded to deal the first hand.

```
Love All                  ♠ A 7 6 3 2
Dealer South              ♥ A J 7 5 3
                          ♦ 5
                          ♣ 5 4
        ♠ 10 8 5                            ♠ 9
        ♥ –              N                  ♥ K 10 9 8 6
        ♦ J 10 9 8    W     E               ♦ Q 6 4 3
        ♣ K J 9 7 6 3    S                  ♣ 10 8 2
                          ♠ K Q J 4
                          ♥ Q 4 2
                          ♦ A K 7 2
                          ♣ A Q
```

WEST	NORTH	EAST	SOUTH
Knight	Parker	Ikonishi	Rufus
–	–	–	2NT
Pass	3♥	Pass	4♠
Pass	5♥	Dble	6♠
All Pass			

'You don't mind if Jonathan and I play conventions such as transfer bids, do you?' Mark Rufus asked.

Ikonishi bowed his head slightly. 'You are most welcome,' he replied. 'My fellow priests do not see the need for them but the outside world contains many imperfections.'

'We're quite happy to play without conventions if you want,' said Rufus.

'No, no, please continue,' replied Ikonishi. 'You are my guests. Most welcome guests.'

Rufus won the jack of diamonds lead with the ace and drew trumps with the king, queen and ace. East, who could not afford to throw a heart, discarded two clubs. When a low heart was led from dummy, Ikonishi played low. South's queen won the trick and West showed out, throwing a club.

Mark Rufus paused to re-assess the situation. There were three heart losers in dummy and he had only one trump in his hand available for ruffing. Relying on the club finesse was not an attractive option. With East holding six major-suit cards to his partner's three, the club finesse was less than a 50% proposition. The best plan was surely to extract East's minor-suit cards, then end-play him in hearts.

Rufus cashed his remaining diamond honour, throwing a club from dummy, then ruffed a diamond. He returned to his hand with the ace of clubs, leaving this end position:

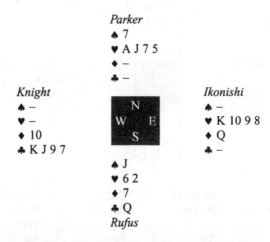

Parker
♠ 7
♥ A J 7 5
♦ —
♣ —

Knight
♠ —
♥ —
♦ 10
♣ K J 9 7

Ikonishi
♠ —
♥ K 10 9 8
♦ Q
♣ —

♠ J
♥ 6 2
♦ 7
♣ Q
Rufus

Since the queen of diamonds had not appeared, it was clear to Rufus that East's last five cards were four hearts and a diamond. He therefore ruffed a diamond in dummy, rather than a club. He then led ♥5, throwing East on lead.

'Admirable play!' congratulated Ikonishi, as he won with the heart eight. His enforced heart return, into the tenace, gave declarer a discard for his losing club. The slam had been made.

Ikonishi laughed. 'I made it very easy for you,' he said. 'When my partner plays the nine on the third round of diamonds, I know it is safe to contribute the queen. You would perhaps then place me with a club and take the wrong ruff.'

Rufus nodded politely. 'Clever idea,' he said. It wouldn't have fooled him, of course. An unknown Japanese priest might or might not have the wit to conceal the ♦6. A wooden player such as Knight would be quite incapable of it, however.

Ikonishi brought the score to Game All with a competently played 3NT, then Rufus had a chance to win the first rubber.

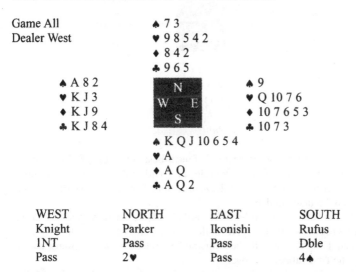

	♠ 7 3		
Game All	♥ 9 8 5 4 2		
Dealer West	♦ 8 4 2		
	♣ 9 6 5		

Hand layout:

North: ♠ 7 3　♥ 9 8 5 4 2　♦ 8 4 2　♣ 9 6 5

West: ♠ A 8 2　♥ K J 3　♦ K J 9　♣ K J 8 4

East: ♠ 9　♥ Q 10 7 6　♦ 10 7 6 5 3　♣ 10 7 3

South: ♠ K Q J 10 6 5 4　♥ A　♦ A Q　♣ A Q 2

WEST	NORTH	EAST	SOUTH
Knight	Parker	Ikonishi	Rufus
1NT	Pass	Pass	Dble
Pass	2♥	Pass	4♠

Knight was somewhat disappointed to open a strong notrump, only to find the opponents reaching game. He led a low trump against Four Spades and Rufus won East's nine with the king. Knight captured the jack of trumps with the ace and exited safely with his last trump.

Rufus paused to consider his continuation. West's 15-17 point opening bid marked East with at most three points. These were likely to include a heart honour, since West would surely have led the suit from a K-Q-J combination. It followed from this that West must hold both the minor-suit kings.

An end-play should be easy enough, thought Rufus. To tighten the eventual end position, he led a low club towards the table. East won dummy's nine with the ten and switched to ♦5. When declarer rose with the ace and ran his remaining trumps, this end position was reached:

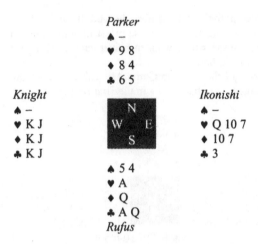

Parker
♠ –
♥ 9 8
♦ 8 4
♣ 6 5

Knight
♠ –
♥ K J
♦ K J
♣ K J

Ikonishi
♠ –
♥ Q 10 7
♦ 10 7
♣ 3

♠ 5 4
♥ A
♦ Q
♣ A Q
Rufus

Knight had noted his partner's fourth-best ♦5 return, followed later by the three. Since this marked declarer with only one more diamond, he released ♦J on the penultimate trump. When the last trump was played, he discarded ♥J.

Rufus was confident how the cards lay. He cashed the ace of hearts, removing West's bare king from the scene, then exited with the diamond queen. Knight won with the king and had to lead back into South's ♣A-Q. The first rubber was over.

Ikonishi caught the declarer's eye. 'You are a strong player, I can tell,' he said. 'Even the way you play each card, it gives the impression of high skill.'

Knight glanced resentfully at Mark Rufus. There hadn't been anything very difficult about the last hand, surely? Anyone could shine if they were given the opportunity.

'Quite humid today,' observed Ikonishi, looking up at the motionless trees. 'You would like some refreshing tea?'

'You mustn't go to all that trouble for us,' replied Knight. 'We don't have too much time, anyway.'

Ikonishi laughed. 'Ah-so, you have been watching National Geographic TV programme on our tea ceremony!' he exclaimed. 'We do not invest our precious time on such matters here. Typhoo pyramid-shape tea bags are quite good enough.'

Some tea was brought to the table and the second rubber began with Ikonishi now partnering Mark Rufus. For the first time the priest had a chance to display his own skills.

Love All
Dealer South

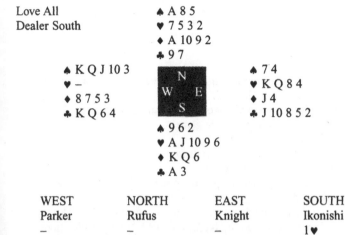

♠ A 8 5
♥ 7 5 3 2
♦ A 10 9 2
♣ 9 7

♠ K Q J 10 3
♥ –
♦ 8 7 5 3
♣ K Q 6 4

♠ 7 4
♥ K Q 8 4
♦ J 4
♣ J 10 8 5 2

♠ 9 6 2
♥ A J 10 9 6
♦ K Q 6
♣ A 3

WEST	NORTH	EAST	SOUTH
Parker	Rufus	Knight	Ikonishi
–	–	–	1♥
1♠	3♥	Pass	4♥

Parker led ♠K against the heart game and Ikonishi won immediately, fearing a singleton in the East hand. A trump to the jack won the next trick, West showing out. Declarer continued with ♥10 to East's queen, retaining his A-9 as a tenace over the king.

Knight returned a spade and Parker cashed two tricks in the suit. Ikonishi won the club king return with the ace and now needed to take all the remaining tricks. It was no easy task. As well as crossing to dummy to take the marked trump finesse, he also needed to score four diamond tricks, to throw his club loser. How could it be done?

It seemed to the Japanese priest that he would need the jack of diamonds to be singleton or doubleton. His next move was a surprising one. He led the king of diamonds, overtaking with dummy's ace. A trump to the nine was followed by the ace of trumps, removing East's last card in the suit. He then cashed the queen of diamonds, laughing happily when the jack fell from East. 'Diamond ten-nine will provide a club discard for me,' he said, facing his remaining cards.

'Neat play!' congratulated Mark Rufus. He stole a quick look at the priest. Hadn't this guy said he was a moderate player?

'Overtaking on the second round of diamonds would be good enough against a doubleton jack,' Ikonishi replied. 'My play wins against single jack, too. East would ruff a second round of diamonds in that case.'

'Quite so,' said Rufus, appreciating the point. 'You played it well.'

A deal or two later, Mark Rufus picked up this hand:

♠ A 2
♥ K 8 4 3
♦ A K 10 7 4 3
♣ 6

With the vulnerability at Game All, Parker opened 3♣ in front of him. 'Three Diamonds,' he said.

The next player passed and Ikonishi responded 3♠. Taking the bid as forcing, Rufus raised to the spade game.

'Four Notrumps,' said Ikonishi.

'What does that mean?' queried Rufus. 'I thought you played natural bidding without any conventions?'

'That is indeed correct,' the priest replied. 'My 4NT is Roman Keycard Blackwood.'

Rufus laughed. 'That doesn't count as a convention, then?' he said.

'There is a precedent for it,' Ikonishi replied. 'In my bridge library I have a book on the 1992 Naturals v Scientists match, written by Terence Reese and his young pupil.'

'Ah, yes,' said Rufus. 'It was played in some big hotel in London, wasn't it?'

'Robson and Forrester, from England, were playing without conventions for the Naturals team. On one hand they used 4NT as Roman Keycard. When the Americans complained, the director ruled it was quite acceptable.'

Rufus laughed. 'It must have been an English tournament director,' he replied. 'Forrester probably slipped him a tenner.'

'Slipped him a tenner?' queried Ikonishi. 'I am not acquainted with this idiom.'

'Gave him ten pounds,' explained Rufus. 'Anyway, if 4NT is Keycard, my bid is Five Hearts.'

This response showed two key-cards (two aces) but no queen of spades. When the priest persisted with 5NT it seemed to Rufus that his diamond suit would offer some play for a grand slam, whatever diamond holding his partner might have. 'Seven Spades,' he said.

This turned out to be the full deal:

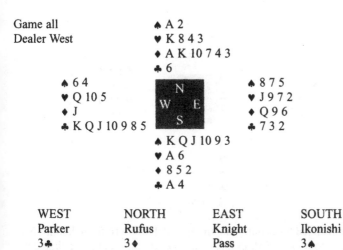

Game all
Dealer West

North:
♠ A 2
♥ K 8 4 3
♦ A K 10 7 4 3
♣ 6

West:
♠ 6 4
♥ Q 10 5
♦ J
♣ K Q J 10 9 8 5

East:
♠ 8 7 5
♥ J 9 7 2
♦ Q 9 6
♣ 7 3 2

South:
♠ K Q J 10 9 3
♥ A 6
♦ 8 5 2
♣ A 4

WEST	NORTH	EAST	SOUTH
Parker	Rufus	Knight	Ikonishi
3♣	3♦	Pass	3♠
Pass	4♠	Pass	4NT
Pass	5♥	Pass	5NT
Pass	7♠	All Pass	

Ikonishi won the king of clubs lead and ruffed his remaining club high, with dummy's ace. He then drew trumps, observing that West had started with two trumps alongside his probable seven clubs. When he crossed to the ace of diamonds, he noted the fall of the jack from West. He returned to his hand with ♥A, West producing the five.

How did the cards lie? If West's shape was 2-2-2-7, the diamond suit would be good and there would be no further problem. What if West had started with 2-3-1-7 shape? In that case East could be caught in a trump squeeze. The Principle of Restricted Choice, to which Ikonishi had devoted considerable study, suggested that the jack of diamonds would be a singleton rather than a chosen card from queen-jack doubleton. Yes, best to play for that chance!

Ikonishi ran his remaining trumps and soon arrived at this five-card ending:

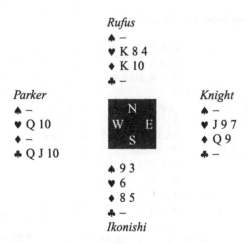

Rufus
♠ —
♥ K 8 4
♦ K 10
♣ —

Parker
♠ —
♥ Q 10
♦ —
♣ Q J 10

Knight
♠ —
♥ J 9 7
♦ Q 9
♣ —

♠ 9 3
♥ 6
♦ 8 5
♣ —
Ikonishi

Ikonishi led his penultimate trump and threw ♦ 10 from dummy. Not wishing to look foolish in this company, Knight spent some time considering his discard. If declarer held one heart and two diamonds, it seemed that he could not avoid giving him an extra trick. If declarer was down to ♥Q6 and a singleton diamond, a diamond discard would beat the slam.

Ikonishi smiled broadly when the nine of diamonds appeared on the table. He crossed to the table's bare king of diamonds, cashed the king of hearts, and returned to his hand with a heart ruff to enjoy the established ♦8.

'You've been fooling us, haven't you?' said Mark Rufus, smiling at the priest. 'You're a good player.'

Ikonishi laughed. 'No difficulty on that one,' he replied.

'Pity I wasn't dealt jack doubleton in diamonds,' continued Parker. 'The jack would have been a good false card on the first round. You might misread the ending after that.'

'Good point,' said Ikonishi. 'You have read the book on squeeze defence by the Vietnamese international, Nguyen Tan Dac?'

'I'm afraid not,' Parker replied.

Suddenly a small wind blew up, disturbing the cards on the table. Ikonishi looked upwards, surveying the sky. 'In ten minutes there will be rain,' he declared. 'Let us go inside for one more rubber. It will be my pleasure to partner Jonathan next, I think.'

The players moved indoors and the priest indicated a circular table that was no more than one foot off the ground. It was surrounded by small cushions, placed on the floor. Knight winced at the sight. It wouldn't do his back much good, sitting on a cushion with no other support.

'We priests normally sit directly on the floor,' observed Ikonishi. 'For your comfort I have placed some cushions, as you see.'

With varying degrees of agility, the four players lowered themselves into a playing position. This was the first deal of the new rubber.

```
Love all              ♠ J 10 4
Dealer South          ♥ 7 6 4 2
                      ♦ Q J 3
                      ♣ A 9 3
     ♠ 8 3                              ♠ A Q 6
     ♥ J 9 3           N                ♥ 10 5
     ♦ A 10 7 4    W       E            ♦ 9 8 5 2
     ♣ K Q J 2         S                ♣ 10 8 7 4
                      ♠ K 9 7 5 2
                      ♥ A K Q 8
                      ♦ K 6
                      ♣ 6 5
```

WEST	NORTH	EAST	SOUTH
Rufus	Knight	Parker	Ikonishi
–	–	–	1♠
Pass	2♠	Pass	3♥
Pass	4♥	End	

Marc Rufus led the king of clubs and Ikonishi played low in the dummy. It did not escape his notice that East followed with ♣8, showing an even number of cards in the suit. When West continued with the club queen, Ikonishi won with dummy's ace. Unless East held a doubleton queen of spades, there was no point in playing on spades now. Dummy's lowly trump spots meant that there would be no subsequent card of re-entry to repeat the finesse.

Instead, Ikonishi made the strange-looking move of ruffing a club at Trick 3. Trumps were drawn in three rounds and declarer then played ♦K. Rufus decided to let this card win. He captured the next round of diamonds and surveyed this position:

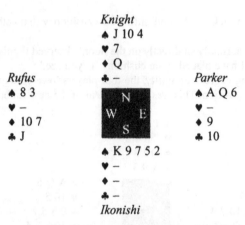

Knight
♠ J 10 4
♥ 7
♦ Q
♣ —

Rufus
♠ 8 3
♥ —
♦ 10 7
♣ J

Parker
♠ A Q 6
♥ —
♦ 9
♣ 10

♠ K 9 7 5 2
♥ —
♦ —
♣ —

Ikonishi

However West defended, declarer would now be able to finesse twice against East's ♠Q. When he chose in fact to play a diamond, Ikonishi won with dummy's queen and played the jack of spades. Parker won with the ace and returned ♣10, ruffed in the dummy. A finesse against the spade queen succeeded and declarer had ten tricks.

'That was amazing,' Rufus exclaimed. 'I think you found the only way to make it. If you play a spade from dummy at Trick 3, I can exit safely in clubs when I take the second diamond.'

Ikonishi smiled. 'An example of lateral thinking,' he said. 'With only one entry to dummy available, and two required, it was necessary to waste the first entry.'

This was the next deal:

North-South Game
Dealer West

♠ 7 4
♥ 9 4
♦ A Q 8 5 3
♣ A Q 5 2

♠ 10 6
♥ K J 10 8 7 6 5 3
♦ 9 6
♣ 3

♠ K 9 3
♥ Q
♦ K J 10 4 2
♣ K J 10 8

♠ A Q J 8 5 2
♥ A 2
♦ 7
♣ 9 7 6 4

WEST	NORTH	EAST	SOUTH
Rufus	Parker	Knight	Ikonishi
4♥	Pass	Pass	4♠
All Pass			

Marc Rufus led his singleton club against the spade game and Ikonishi leaned forward to play the ace from dummy. A finesse of the trump queen succeeded and he re-entered dummy with the ace of diamonds to repeat the trump finesse.

After drawing East's last trump with the ace, Ikonishi cashed the ace of hearts to remove East's holding in the suit. He had not yet lost a trick and this position had been reached:

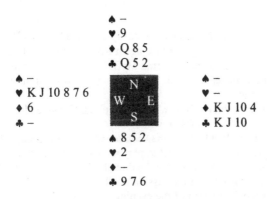

```
                    ♠ –
                    ♥ 9
                    ♦ Q 8 5
                    ♣ Q 5 2
   ♠ –                              ♠ –
   ♥ K J 10 8 7 6      N            ♥ –
   ♦ 6              W     E         ♦ K J 10 4
   ♣ –                S             ♣ K J 10
                    ♠ 8 5 2
                    ♥ 2
                    ♦ –
                    ♣ 9 7 6
```

Ikonishi now ducked a club to the East hand. Rupert Knight viewed the dummy's holdings unhappily. When he eventually led the king of diamonds. Ikonishi declined to ruff, preferring to throw his heart loser. 'I just make one more trick, then,' said Knight, facing his remaining cards. 'You played it well. Very well indeed.'

Not long afterwards, the three Englishmen were bidding their farewells to the remarkable Japanese priest. 'Most kind of you to visit such an old man,' Ikonishi declared. 'I have made a note of your excellent phrase "slipped him a tenner". I hope to use it very soon.'

'I'm sorry we couldn't give you a chance to practise your Albanian,' said Knight, as he shook the priest by the hand.

Ikonishi laughed. 'You gave me a chance to practise my bridge,' he replied. 'A more useful skill, I think!

7

Rupert Knight's Scottish Connection

The King Harald II was making steady progress towards Bali as the after-dinner duplicate began. Once again Knight had been landed with a less than optimal partner - Norma McBain, the Scotswoman.

'Most unfortunate,' she said. 'Ailsa ate some bad sushi in Osaka and can't play tonight.'

'That's very unlucky for her,' Knight replied. 'No-one else seems to have had any problems of that nature.'

'I meant it was bad luck for me,' continued Norma McBain. 'I didn't pay a fortune for this cruise just to play with a strange partner.'

Knight bit his lip. Silly old bat, he thought. If she didn't want to play with him, why turn up for the session at all?

This was the first board of the evening:

```
North-South game        ♠ 7 6 3
Dealer West             ♥ 3
                        ♦ J 7 6 4 2
                        ♣ A Q 3 2
  ♠ K Q J 10 9 4 2    N            ♠ 5
  ♥ 10 5                           ♥ A Q 9 7 6
  ♦ 8 3           W        E       ♦ Q 10 9 5
  ♣ 8 5               S            ♣ 9 6 4
                        ♠ A 8
                        ♥ K J 8 4 2
                        ♦ A K
                        ♣ K J 10 7
```

WEST	NORTH	EAST	SOUTH
Giles	Norma	Felicity	Rupert
C-Browne	McBain	C-Browne	Knight
3♠	Pass	Pass	3NT
All Pass			

Rupert Knight was uncertain what to bid when West's pre-emptive 3♠ ran to him. An expert panel would probably have divided their votes between 3NT, 4♥ and Double. The advantage of 3NT was that it might be playable even when there was a heart fit. If he gambled on 4♥ and dummy went down with a shortage in the suit, there would be no way back. 'Three Notrumps,' said Knight.

Giles Couttes-Browne, whose dinner suit was impressive by anyone's standards, led the king of spades.

'You should make it easily,' declared Norma McBain, spreading the dummy. 'I have seven extra points for you.'

Knight ducked the first round of spades and won the next, East throwing a heart. With only seven top tricks, it seemed that he would have to make something of the diamonds. He cashed the ace and king of the suit, both defenders following, and continued with the king and jack of clubs. He then crossed to the queen of clubs and led ♦J. East won with the queen and West showed out, throwing a spade.

Felicity Couttes-Browne was now in some trouble. Had declarer not removed her clubs, she could have exited safely in that suit, beating the contract. What should she do? It would be hopeless to cash her remaining diamond winner, setting up a long diamond in dummy. She therefore switched to a low heart. Since Knight still had only seven tricks available outside hearts, he had to try the jack of hearts. He breathed a sigh of relief when this card held. He returned to dummy with the ace of clubs, leaving these cards still to be played:

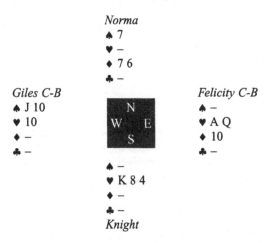

Norma
♠ 7
♥ —
♦ 7 6
♣ —

Giles C-B
♠ J 10
♥ 10
♦ —
♣ —

Felicity C-B
♠ —
♥ A Q
♦ 10
♣ —

Knight
♠ —
♥ K 8 4
♦ —
♣ —

'Play the diamond,' instructed Knight.

With an aggravated shrug of the shoulders, Felicity Couttes-Browne had to win the diamond trick and play the ace and queen of hearts. The heart king was declarer's ninth trick and the game had been made.

Knight beamed happily at his partner. What a play it had been!

'You made hard work of that,' Norma McBain declared. 'You bid game on your own hand and I gave you seven extra points.'

Consoled by the +600 on his card, Knight managed to maintain a pleasant disposition. Had the Scotswoman not attended his lecture on protective bidding? Next time she would put down a one-count and claim she had given him something extra.

This was the next board:

```
East-West game          ♠ 7 5 4
Dealer South            ♥ 9 5
                        ♦ A 8 6 2
                        ♣ K 6 3 2
        ♠ K J 2              N          ♠ 10
        ♥ K Q J 8                       ♥ 10 7 6 3
        ♦ K Q 10 3      W        E      ♦ J 9 5 4
        ♣ Q 9               S          ♣ J 10 7 4
                        ♠ A Q 9 8 6 3
                        ♥ A 4 2
                        ♦ 7
                        ♣ A 8 5
```

WEST	NORTH	EAST	SOUTH
Giles	Norma	Felicity	Rupert
C-Browne	McBain	C-Browne	Knight
–	–	–	1♠
1NT	2♠	Pass	4♠
All Pass			

Rupert Knight was conscious that his 4♠ was an overbid. Partners such as Norma were usually subdued by an opposing 1NT overcall, however, and he was expecting fair values in the dummy. Giles Couttes-Browne adjusted his gold-rimmed spectacles, then led the king of hearts.

'Two good cards for you, partner,' observed Norma, as she lay down the dummy.

Knight nodded his thanks. Prospects were not good and if the contract went down he would have to take the blame himself. There was a certain loser in both hearts and clubs and West's 1NT overcall strongly suggested two trump losers too. What could be done?

Knight's first move was to duck the opening lead. This would prevent East from gaining the lead on the second round of hearts and maybe playing a trump through the ace-queen. Still on lead at Trick 2, Giles Couttes-Browne switched to the king of diamonds. 'Ace, please,' said Knight.

A diamond ruff in hand was followed by the ace of hearts and a heart ruff in dummy. When Knight ruffed a second diamond, the nine appeared from East and the ten from West. Still uncertain of the line he would eventually take, Knight cashed the ace of clubs and crossed to dummy with the club king. This position had been reached:

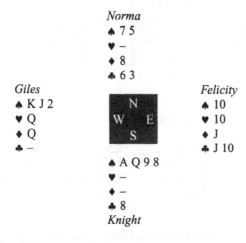

Norma
♠ 7 5
♥ –
♦ 8
♣ 6 3

Giles
♠ K J 2
♥ Q
♦ Q
♣ –

Felicity
♠ 10
♥ 10
♦ J
♣ J 10

♠ A Q 9 8
♥ –
♦ –
♣ 8
Knight

If West had started with 2-4-4-3 or 2-4-5-2 shape, the winning line now would be to play ace and another trump. However, neither of these distributions would make a 1NT overcall attractive.

Knight was inclined to place West with an original 3-4-4-2 shape. He called for another diamond and ruffed with the eight, pleased to see both defenders follow suit. When Knight exited with ♣8, West discarded his last heart and East won the trick. Knight ruffed the club continuation with the nine, then faced his last two cards, the ace and queen of trumps. 'If you overruff, you'll have to lead back into my tenace,' he said.

Giles Couttes-Browne returned his cards to the wallet, then looked triumphantly across the table. 'I judged that one well!' he exclaimed. 'Most people would have doubled Four Spades on my hand.'

'What a pity you didn't,' said Norma McBain. 'That would have been a nice top for us.'

Knight could scarcely believe that no comment had been passed on his dummy play. Plus 420 would surely be a 'nice top for us', he thought. There was no need to bemoan the lack of a double.

Norma McBain peered through her spectacles at the travelling score-sheet. 'It is a good one for us, actually,' she said. 'I don't know why.'

A round of two later, Knight and his partner faced Rufus and Parker.

```
Love All                    ♠ 7 5 4 3
Dealer West                 ♥ 10
                            ♦ A K Q 5
                            ♣ Q 9 8 4
        ♠ J                                 ♠ Q 10 8 6
        ♥ K J 8 7 6 4 3        N            ♥ Q 2
        ♦ J 10 6 4         W       E        ♦ 9 8 2
        ♣ 5                   S            ♣ K 10 7 2
                            ♠ A K 9 2
                            ♥ A 9 5
                            ♦ 7 3
                            ♣ A J 6 3
```

WEST	NORTH	EAST	SOUTH
Rupert	Jonathan	Norma	Mark
Knight	Parker	McBain	Rufus
3♥	Dble	Pass	6♠
All Pass			

Knight led his singleton club and Parker, somewhat shamefacedly, put down the dummy. 'Bit of a joke, I'm afraid,' he said. 'Only eleven points but I thought you might be stuck for a bid if I passed.'

'It's fine,' Rufus replied. 'Play the nine, will you?'

Norma McBain covered with ♣10 and Rufus won with the jack. The ace of trumps dropped the jack from West at Trick 2. What now, thought Rufus? The king of clubs was surely onside, so if trumps were

3-2 all would be easy. Could he handle a 4-1 trump break? It wasn't easy to calculate. There was a fair bit of work to do.

Rufus cashed the ace of hearts and ruffed a heart, the queen appearing from East. It seemed to him that if trumps were 4-1 he could not afford to play a trump at this stage. East would doubtless split her honours and there would not be enough entries to dummy to achieve everything that was needed. 'Queen of clubs, please,' said Rufus.

The queen was covered by the king and ace. When West showed out but was unable to ruff, Rufus breathed a sigh of relief. Trumps were obviously 4-1 but he might be able to cope with the situation. He crossed to dummy with the ace of diamonds and called for a trump. East put in the queen and he won with the king.

Rufus returned to dummy with the king of diamonds and threw a club on the diamond queen. This end position had been reached:

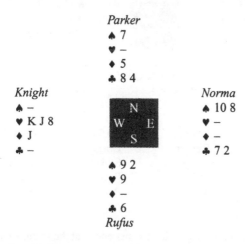

```
                      Parker
                      ♠ 7
                      ♥ —
                      ♦ 5
                      ♣ 8 4
      Knight                            Norma
      ♠ —              N                ♠ 10 8
      ♥ K J 8      W       E            ♥ —
      ♦ J              S                ♦ —
      ♣ —                               ♣ 7 2
                      ♠ 9 2
                      ♥ 9
                      ♦ —
                      ♣ 6
                      Rufus
```

The five of diamonds was led and there was nothing that Norma McBain could do. When she decided to throw a club, Rufus ruffed with the two and returned to dummy with ♣8. A lead of dummy's last club then allowed him to score his ♠9 en passant.

Knight reached for his score-card, inserting a large zero in the estimate column. 'Is it better if Norma doesn't cover the club queen?' he said. 'You can't get back to dummy with the eight, then.'

'Makes no difference,' Rufus replied. 'I can lead a trump from dummy and duck when the queen comes. Then I win the diamond return in dummy and pick up the trumps.'

Knight struggled to follow this. 'You still have another loser, don't you?' he said. 'You can't ruff the second heart and there's a slow loser in clubs.'

'I think you'll find the third round of clubs squeezes you in the red suits,' Rufus replied. 'It was the opening lead that cost it. I don't think I can make it on any other lead.'

'Yes, that lead ruined my club holding,' said Norma. She gave a sad shake of the head. 'It's been much the same all evening.'

The final round brought less intimidating opposition to Knight's table, Doris Stokes and the football-shirted Oakley Hampton.

```
Love All                  ♠ A K 2
Dealer North              ♥ 8 4
                          ♦ Q 10 8 6
                          ♣ A 9 4 2
        ♠ 10 9 8 4                        ♠ Q J 7 3
        ♥ J 10 7 6          N             ♥ 2
        ♦ 9 4          W         E        ♦ K 7 5 3 2
        ♣ Q 10 3           S             ♣ J 7 5
                          ♠ 6 5
                          ♥ A K Q 9 5 3
                          ♦ A J
                          ♣ K 8 6
```

WEST	NORTH	EAST	SOUTH
Oakley	Rupert	Doris	Norma
Hampton	Knight	Stokes	McBain
–	1NT	Pass	4♣
Pass	4♠	Pass	6♥
All Pass			

Knight groaned inwardly as his partner ended at the helm. He had no great liking for Gerber, anyway. Couldn't she at least have preceded it with a transfer response, letting him play the hand?

Hampton led ♠10 and Norma won in the dummy. When she continued with two top trumps, East showed out on the second round. 'Oh, dear,' Norma exclaimed. 'That's very unlucky.'

She drew a third round of trumps, then crossed to the king of spades and played a diamond to the jack. The finesse succeeded but the contract was still in trouble. Norma exited with a trump, ruffed the spade return, then ran her remaining trumps, hoping that something good would happen. It was not to be. Doris maintained a determined guard on her king of diamonds and the slam was one down.

'Trumps always seem to break 4-1 when I bid a slam,' Norma declared. 'It was a really good hand for Gerber, too.'

Knight gritted his teeth. If the old dear was expecting a 4-1 trump break, why not lead a diamond to the jack at Trick 2? She could then play three top trumps, discovering the break, and cash ♦ A. Two entries would remain to take a ruffing finesse in diamonds and to reach the established winner if East covered on the third round.

'Nothing I could do,' Norma declared. 'I did my best at the end there, playing for a... you know, one of those squeezes.'

'Yes,' replied Rupert Knight. 'It was a clever effort.'

Knight could not believe it when on the very next deal Norma arrived in another slam, a grand slam no less. A confirmed non-believer, he nevertheless uttered a small prayer. Please let the suits break well, so that Norma could make the contract. He would never hear the end of it, otherwise.

East-West game	♠ K Q 7 4	
Dealer East	♥ 6 5	
	♦ A K Q 8 5 4	
	♣ 6	

♠ 5		♠ 10 8 6 2
♥ Q 9 3		♥ J 10 4
♦ J 10 6 2		♦ 9
♣ 10 8 7 5 4		♣ K Q J 3 2

♠ A J 9 3
♥ A K 8 7 2
♦ 7 3
♣ A 9

WEST	NORTH	EAST	SOUTH
Oakley	Rupert	Doris	Norma
Hampton	Knight	Stokes	McBain
–	–	Pass	1♥
Pass	2♦	Pass	2♠
Pass	4♣	Dble	4NT
Pass	7♠	All Pass	

When Norma admitted to three aces, in response to his Gerber enquiry, Knight could visualise an easy grand slam. Norma won the club lead with the ace and played the ace of trumps, both defenders following. When she played a second trump to the king, West showed out.

'It probably won't cost on this occasion,' muttered Norma, 'but it's rather annoying when you always get a 4-1 trump break.'

Trumps were drawn in two more rounds and Norma then turned to the diamond suit. She could not believe it when this suit, too, proved to be 4-1. The grand slam was three down.

'This is the worst bridge cruise I've ever been on!' Norma exclaimed. 'Two perfect bidding sequences and we end up with two bottoms.'

'Only because my partner defended so cleverly,' Doris remarked. 'You did well to hold on to those diamonds, Oakley.'

'I wasn't letting one of those go,' Hampton replied proudly. 'In any case, I was inspired by the way you held on to your diamonds on the previous hand.'

Gritting his teeth yet again, Knight inserted the minus score onto the traveller. He could hardly point it out, but once again she might have made the slam. When trumps proved to be 4-1, she could have cashed two top hearts and ruffed a heart with the queen. With the heart suit breaking 3-3, she could have taken the marked finesse of ♠9, drawn the last trump, and claimed the contract. If hearts did not prove to be 3-3, she could still have fallen back on a 3-2 diamond break.

Doris turned towards Rupert Knight. 'You see how well Oakley and I play together?' she said. 'We always seem to be on the same wavelength in defence.'

'That's the first piece of good news I've had all evening,' said Knight, summoning his bridge organiser's smile. 'Do you hear that, Norma? Two happy customers!'

8

Stacked Deal in Bali

The cruise ship had anchored off Bali for a one-night stay and the passengers were about to board the tender to take them ashore.

Rupert Knight was surprised to see that Debbie and Sharon were unattended. 'You're not going with Marc and Jonathan?' he said.

'No,' Debbie replied. 'The boys are going surfing. Do you want to walk round with us?'

Knight needed no second invitation. The first forty years of his life had brought him little success with females and a few hours in the company of two pretty girls was a prize well worth grasping. 'Excellent idea,' he replied.

It was hot and humid in Denpasar, the island's capital. The local beach had been crowded and the three were soon wandering in search of a cool bar. 'All day brekfast. Egg's, bacon's, tost, jam. Only 1200Rh' offered one establishment. The place was packed out with tourists, so Knight and the girls decided to walk further. 'Back-pack accomodation with own bed, very good comfort. 2000Rh!!' was on offer at a nearby hostel.

'What's the local currency?' asked Sharon.

'The Indonesian rupiah,' Knight responded. 'A thousand rupiah to the pound, near enough. Everything seems very cheap here.'

Debbie, whose bar selection criteria had diminished with each sun-baked step, pointed across the road. 'That place looks good,' she said. 'Let's give it a try.'

Three glasses of the local beer, well chilled, worked wonders. In the far corner of the bar there were two groups of youngsters playing cards. 'Don't know what game they're playing on the left table, there,' said Knight. 'Looks like bridge on the right. Can't get away from it!.'

They wandered over to take a look, just as this hand was being dealt:

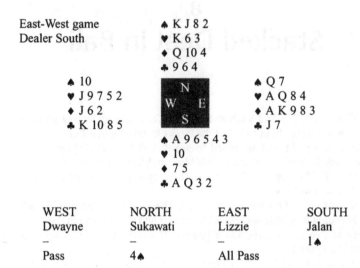

East-West game
Dealer South

♠ K J 8 2
♥ K 6 3
♦ Q 10 4
♣ 9 6 4

♠ 10
♥ J 9 7 5 2
♦ J 6 2
♣ K 10 8 5

♠ Q 7
♥ A Q 8 4
♦ A K 9 8 3
♣ J 7

♠ A 9 6 5 4 3
♥ 10
♦ 7 5
♣ A Q 3 2

WEST	NORTH	EAST	SOUTH
Dwayne	Sukawati	Lizzie	Jalan
–	–	–	1♠
Pass	4♠	All Pass	

Sitting East and West were two young Australians, bronzed by the sun until they were almost as dark as the local youths they were playing against. Two bids carried the auction to 4♠ and the blonde-haired girl in the East seat was frozen out of the auction, despite holding the best hand at the table.

The West player, who was clad only in shorts, the better to display his well-toned surfer's body, led ♣5.

'Only worth Three Spades, maybe,' observed Sukawati, as he laid out the dummy.

Debbie leaned forward, her blonde hair brushing against Knight's ear. 'I would only bid Two Spades on his hand,' she whispered. 'He's got ten losers, if you count one extra for no aces.'

Declarer won East's jack with the queen and drew trumps in two rounds. Prospects were fairly hopeless but he could see one small chance. He cashed the ace of clubs, removing East's last card in the suit, then played a diamond to the ten.

The Australian girl won with the king and was hopelessly endplayed. If she cashed her remaining two winners in the red suits, she would set up two discards for declarer's club losers. After a few moments she cashed just the ace of diamonds, then exited with a diamond to dummy's queen. This defence would have succeeded if declarer had started with 6-2-3-2 shape. As it was, he was able to discard his singleton heart. An eventual club ruff then brought him a tenth trick.

'Don't think much of that lead, Dwayne,' complained the young blonde, who had a very twangy Australian accent. 'Only lead to give it to him, wasn't it?'

Dwayne took a dismissive swig from his bottle of Foster's. 'I'm not leading from a jack and I never lead a singleton trump,' he replied, proceeding to wipe his mouth with the back of his hand. 'Nothing wrong with leading from a king-ten. It works fine, normally.'

This was the next hand:

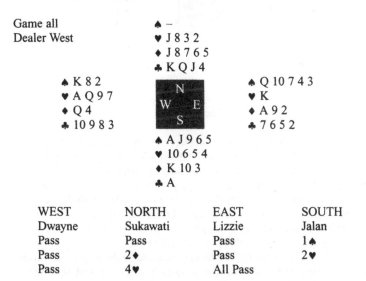

Game all
Dealer West

North hand:
♠ —
♥ J 8 3 2
♦ J 8 7 6 5
♣ K Q J 4

West hand:
♠ K 8 2
♥ A Q 9 7
♦ Q 4
♣ 10 9 8 3

East hand:
♠ Q 10 7 4 3
♥ K
♦ A 9 2
♣ 7 6 5 2

South hand:
♠ A J 9 6 5
♥ 10 6 5 4
♦ K 10 3
♣ A

WEST	NORTH	EAST	SOUTH
Dwayne	Sukawati	Lizzie	Jalan
Pass	Pass	Pass	1♠
Pass	2♦	Pass	2♥
Pass	4♥	All Pass	

West led ♣10 and down went the dummy. Once more Debbie leaned towards Rupert Knight. 'I wouldn't bid Four Hearts on that, would you?' she whispered. 'Serves him right that they got too high.'

Jalan won with the ace of clubs and reached dummy with a spade ruff. Three more rounds of clubs stood up and he discarded all three of his diamonds. A diamond ruff in hand was followed by the ace of spades and a spade ruff in dummy. A second diamond ruff in the South hand left this four-card end position:

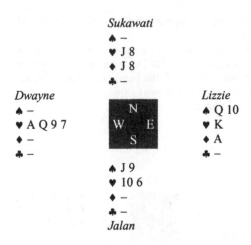

Sukawati
♠ –
♥ J 8
♦ J 8
♣ –

Dwayne
♠ –
♥ A Q 9 7
♦ –
♣ –

Lizzie
♠ Q 10
♥ K
♦ A
♣ –

♠ J 9
♥ 10 6
♦ –
♣ –
Jalan

With one trick still needed, declarer led a spade from his hand. Dwayne ruffed in with the queen and led a low trump to his partner's king, leaving declarer with just one trump in each hand. Fortunately for him, East had no further trump to play. When she returned the ace of diamonds, Jalan ruffed with the ten. West overruffed with the ace and dummy's jack of trumps was now good for a tenth trick.

'He shouldn't make that!' Lizzie exclaimed. 'Lead a diamond and I make my ace. We've got three trump tricks to come.'

'Jeez, you want me to lead from queen-one in dummy's suit?' cried Dwayne. He counted off a few bank notes from a large wad, settling his losses on the rubber, then beckoned for the barman to bring him another beer.

The North player stood up. 'I mus' going back to kitchen now,' he said. 'Meal break over.'

Jalan was gathering in the cards as Rupert Knight stepped forward. 'Can I take his place?' he said.

'We were playing bridge,' Jalan replied. 'You know it?'

'Sure do,' said Knight. 'What stakes do you play for.'

The good-looking Jalan laughed. 'Only 100 rupiah,' he said. 'My backpacker friends here bid on every hand unless we have some kind of stake.'

The game restarted with Knight in partnership with Jalan. This was an early deal:

Love All
Dealer South

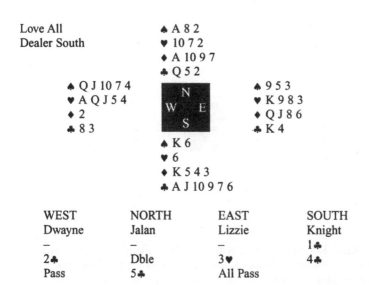

```
                    ♠ A 8 2
                    ♥ 10 7 2
                    ♦ A 10 9 7
                    ♣ Q 5 2
     ♠ Q J 10 7 4          ♠ 9 5 3
     ♥ A Q J 5 4           ♥ K 9 8 3
     ♦ 2                   ♦ Q J 8 6
     ♣ 8 3                 ♣ K 4
                    ♠ K 6
                    ♥ 6
                    ♦ K 5 4 3
                    ♣ A J 10 9 7 6
```

WEST	NORTH	EAST	SOUTH
Dwayne	Jalan	Lizzie	Knight
–	–	–	1♣
2♣	Dble	3♥	4♣
Pass	5♣	All Pass	

Dwayne entered the auction with a Michaels cue-bid, showing both major suits. Knight stretched to a 4♣ rebid and was raised to game by his young partner. West thumbed through his cards uncertainly. Should he lead the diamond or a top spade? Better make the right choice or Lizzie would let off steam again. Eventually he tossed ♦2 onto the table.

Knight won with dummy's ace of diamonds and led the queen of trumps, covered by the king and ace. After drawing trumps with a second round, he exited with ♥6, won by West's jack. The Australian could sense that a heart continuation might assist declarer towards an elimination ending. He switched to the queen of spades instead, declarer winning with the king.

Knight paused to consider his continuation. If he could reduce East to just her three remaining diamonds, a throw-in would be possible. It was not easy to see how this could be done. Maybe she would run out of discards if the trumps were run.

Knight cashed three more rounds of trumps, arriving at this position:

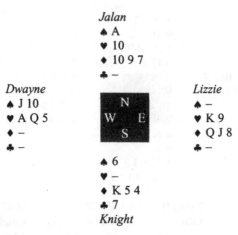

Jalan
♠ A
♥ 10
♦ 10 9 7
♣ —

Dwayne
♠ J 10
♥ A Q 5
♦ —
♣ —

Lizzie
♠ —
♥ K 9
♦ Q J 8
♣ —

♠ 6
♥ —
♦ K 5 4
♣ 7

Knight

When Knight continued with a spade to the ace, Lizzie could not afford to discard a diamond. She had to release one of her hearts and Knight promptly ruffed a heart, removing her last card in the suit.

With the North, East and South hands all down to three diamonds, the hard work had been done. A diamond to the ten threw East on lead and she had to play away from her remaining diamond honour. Declarer had eleven tricks.

'That was good play!' exclaimed Jalan. He gave a boyish laugh. 'I am embarrassed that I asked just now whether you knew the game.'

Knight was called into action again on the very next deal:

North-South game
Dealer West

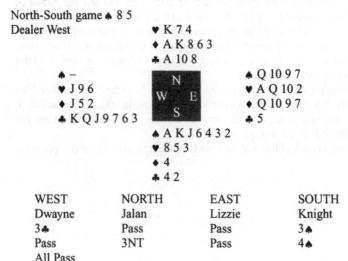

♠ 8 5
♥ K 7 4
♦ A K 8 6 3
♣ A 10 8

♠ —
♥ J 9 6
♦ J 5 2
♣ K Q J 9 7 6 3

♠ Q 10 9 7
♥ A Q 10 2
♦ Q 10 9 7
♣ 5

♠ A K J 6 4 3 2
♥ 8 5 3
♦ 4
♣ 4 2

WEST	NORTH	EAST	SOUTH
Dwayne	Jalan	Lizzie	Knight
3♣	Pass	Pass	3♠
Pass	3NT	Pass	4♠
All Pass			

Perhaps himself influenced by the 100 rupiah stake, Jalan decided that he was not quite worth a 3 ♦ overcall. Knight protected with 3 ♠ and Dwayne led the king of clubs against the eventual spade game.

Knight won in the dummy and played a trump to the jack. The finesse succeeded but West showed out, leaving declarer with a trump loser. The heart ace was sure to be offside after West's non-vulnerable pre-empt, so it was not easy to see how ten tricks might be made. Perhaps a throw-in would be possible.

Knight drew two more rounds of trumps, leaving East with a master, then cashed two rounds of diamonds, throwing a club. A diamond ruff in his hand left these cards outstanding:

Jalan
♠ –
♥ K 7 4
♦ 8 6
♣ 10

Dwayne
♠ –
♥ J 9 6
♦ –
♣ Q J 9

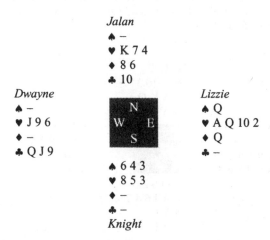

Lizzie
♠ Q
♥ A Q 10 2
♦ Q
♣ –

♠ 6 4 3
♥ 8 5 3
♦ –
♣ –

Knight

Knight exited with a trump to East's queen. When the Australian girl returned the queen of diamonds, he discarded a heart instead of ruffing. She now had to play on hearts, surrendering a tenth trick to dummy's king of hearts.

'No need to tell me,' said Dwayne. 'It was totally obvious to lead a heart from the jack, I realise.'

Lizzie tossed back her somewhat unruly head of sun-bleached hair. 'Did I say a word?' she said.

Knight cast a discerning eye over the two Australians. Were they romantically linked? If so, it didn't look like an arrangement that would last very long.

'I knew what you were thinking, though,' Dwayne replied. 'Pity you weren't sitting over here, really. You would have made all the right leads, I'm sure.'

The Australian girl rose to her feet. 'That's enough. I'm off to the beach,' she declared, peeling off a few rupiah bills and dropping them on the table. 'It was a stupid idea in the first place, playing bridge when the sun's shining.'

'I'm all for that,' Dwayne declared. He retrieved a well-worn surf board from behind the bar and the two headed out into the sunshine.

Jalan looked across at Knight. 'Your two girlfriends play bridge?' he queried.

'Thought you'd never ask!' exclaimed Debbie, slipping into one of the vacant seats.

Debbie and Sharon won the first rubber, after several light-hearted exchanges. A few deals into the second rubber, the young Jalan had a chance to restore the balance.

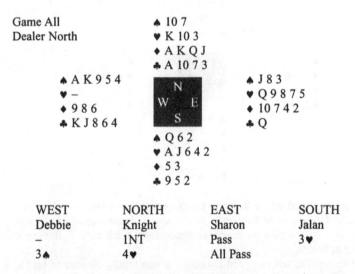

Game All
Dealer North

North:
♠ 10 7
♥ K 10 3
♦ A K Q J
♣ A 10 7 3

West:
♠ A K 9 5 4
♥ –
♦ 9 8 6
♣ K J 8 6 4

East:
♠ J 8 3
♥ Q 9 8 7 5
♦ 10 7 4 2
♣ Q

South:
♠ Q 6 2
♥ A J 6 4 2
♦ 5 3
♣ 9 5 2

WEST	NORTH	EAST	SOUTH
Debbie	Knight	Sharon	Jalan
–	1NT	Pass	3♥
3♠	4♥	All Pass	

Debbie cashed two top spades against the heart game, her partner playing the three and the eight to signal three cards in the suit. She then paused for thought. Since declarer had responded 3♥ rather than 4♥, there was a fair chance that he held only five trumps. In that case, Sharon would have five trumps too. Hoping to attack dummy's trumps and reduce declarer's finessing potential in the suit, Debbie played a third round of spades. Unfortunately for her, it was South who produced the spade queen, winning the trick.

A trump to the king revealed the 5-0 break and Jalan continued with four rounds of diamonds, discarding two clubs. The ace of clubs came next, leaving this end position:

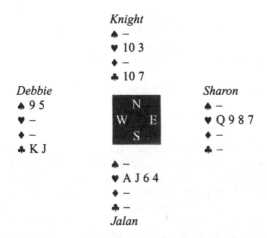

Knight
♠ –
♥ 10 3
♦ –
♣ 10 7

Debbie
♠ 9 5
♥ –
♦ –
♣ K J

Sharon
♠ –
♥ Q 9 8 7
♦ –
♣ –

♠ –
♥ A J 6 4
♦ –
♣ –
Jalan

When a club was led from dummy, Sharon ruffed with the nine. Jalan was not tempted to overruff with the jack. He underruffed with the four and faced his remaining cards. 'Three trump tricks to me?' he said.

Sharon studied the layout of the trump suit in disbelief. 'That's amazing,' she said. 'I was sure you were going down, there.'

Rupert Knight thought back over the early play. 'It wasn't easy for you, Debbie,' he said, 'but I think a club switch at Trick 3 might have worked better. It's difficult for declarer to cash the queen of spades, then.'

'I still make it, I think' said Jalan. He restored the cards to their original positions, then played them off one by one. The king of trumps, exposing the break, was followed by three rounds of diamonds. This, slightly different, end position lay before them:

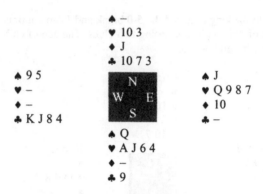

♠ –
♥ 10 3
♦ J
♣ 10 7 3

♠ 9 5
♥ –
♦ –
♣ K J 8 4

N
W E
S

♠ J
♥ Q 9 8 7
♦ 10
♣ –

♠ Q
♥ A J 6 4
♦ –
♣ 9

'You see what I mean?' said Knight. 'You throw your last club on the diamond, but when you play a club, Sharon can ruff in. It won't do you any good to duck then, because she would have a safe exit in spades.'

Jalan smiled. 'That defence beats it, then?' he said

'Sure does,' replied Knight triumphantly.

'Not so, I would trump the last diamond winner!' exclaimed Jalan. 'Then I cash the spade queen and exit with a club. East has to ruff and lead away from the queen of trumps.'

Knight blinked. What was this guy doing, playing for peanut stakes in some backpackers bar? He was a stronger performer than any of them. 'Where on earth did you learn to play like that?' he enquired.

The Balinese youth smiled. 'Colorado State,' he replied.

Debbie's mouth fell open. 'What, in America?' she said.

'That's right,' Jalan replied. 'I just finished my masters in Electrical Engineering.'

Knight could not believe what he was hearing. This guy, who looked no more than about seventeen, had achieved more than he had in all his forty years. He had a degree, for a start. He was more good-looking than anyone could wish for, and he already played bridge like a champion.

'Ah, here is Prasanna!' Jalan exclaimed, his eyes shining brightly. 'She would very much like to meet you all, I'm sure.'

Knight could barely steel himself to look round. Unless he was very much mistaken, some splendid Balinese girlfriend was about to appear on the scene. The great Dealer in the Sky certainly liked to drop all the aces in one place. Didn't he realise how unfair that was?

9

Mitzi Sucherman's Lucky Day

Marc Rufus was perspiring heavily as he emerged from the ship's gymnasium. 'No game tonight, then?' he asked, as he bumped into Rupert Knight.

Knight surveyed Rufus with a look of total amazement. Why on earth did sane people volunteer to put themselves through agonies on devices such as weight-lifting machines? He himself had never entered a gym since leaving school. His figure wasn't the best, it was true, and he had gained a couple of stone in the last year or so. In fact, come to think of it, perhaps it would be a good idea if he worked out a bit. He might have more luck with women, for one thing. 'No,' he replied. 'Everyone wanted to go to the damn silly entertainment evening put on by the ship's staff.'

'We could have a few rubbers, just four of us,' suggested Rufus. 'Cutting for partners, of course. I'm sure Sucherman would be willing.'

'What sort of stake are you thinking of?' asked Knight.

'Just enough to keep the game honest,' Rufus replied. 'Five pounds a 100?'

Knight blanched. 'A two-pound game is high enough for me,' he declared. 'You and Jonathan can play for fives when you're on opposite sides.'

'Done!' exclaimed Rufus. 'See you in the card-room after dinner.'

That night the cruise dinner was as excellent as always. Six courses, if you took them all, starting with crab and prawn mousse, then game soup and croutons, lemon sole in a sauce Anglaise, pheasant casserole, almond ice cream, and a French cheeseboard. Normally Knight would have enjoyed every moment of the meal. On this occasion his mind was elsewhere. If you had a really bad session you could lose quite a lot, even at two-pound stakes. Perhaps he shouldn't be drinking wine? Alcohol never did much to improve his game. He glanced across to the table that Mark and Jonathan shared with Debbie and Sharon. They certainly weren't holding back! The bottle the waiter had just brought to their table was surely the third between four people. Pity he couldn't have arranged to be on the same table as Debbie and Sharon himself.

'Penny for your thoughts,' said Vera Stoute. 'Which one of those girls is your favourite?'

Knight laughed nervously. 'Debbie and Sharon, do you mean?' he replied. 'I wasn't looking at them. I was er... looking for a waiter to bring us some coffee.'

'It's on the table already,' Vera replied.

'Ah good,' said Knight. 'Just what I need before the big game tonight.'

Twenty minutes later the game was about to start. Knight and Sucherman would play for two-pound stakes throughout. Rufus and Parker would play for five pounds when they faced each other.

Knight cut to play with Parker on the first rubber and this was the first deal:

```
Love All              ♠ A K 8 3
Dealer South          ♥ 7 6 4
                      ♦ K Q 9 6 2
                      ♣ A
     ♠ J 7 4                         ♠ Q 9 6
     ♥ J                N            ♥ Q 10 8 2
     ♦ 8 4          W       E        ♦ J 10 7
     ♣ K Q 10 9 6 5 3      S         ♣ 8 7 4
                      ♠ 10 5 2
                      ♥ A K 9 5 3
                      ♦ A 5 3
                      ♣ J 2
```

WEST	NORTH	EAST	SOUTH
Mark	Jonathan	Ralph	Rupert
Rufus	Parker	Sucherman	Knight
–	–	–	1♥
3♣	4♣	Pass	4♦
Pass	6♥	All Pass	

Knight was uncertain whether he should cue-bid his ace of diamonds. He had three big cards, it was true, but only twelve points. With stakes this high, and knowing his luck, whatever he did was likely to turn out wrong. A few seconds later he was installed in Six Hearts and Rufus led ♣K.

Parker smiled across the table. 'Don't know how high you play negative doubles,' he said. 'Thought I'd better play safe and agree hearts.'

Knight won with dummy's ace of clubs and played a trump to the ace, the jack falling from West. There was every chance of a 4-1 trump break, so he returned to dummy with a top spade and led another trump, intending to put in the nine. Sucherman thwarted this by rising with the queen. Knight captured with the king and West showed out, discarding a club.

Knight paused to recalculate his position. If he ruffed his club loser there would be no way to neutralise East's 10-8 of trumps. It seemed that he would need to find East with at least three diamonds.

When three rounds of diamonds were played, the news was good - East followed all the way. This position had been reached:

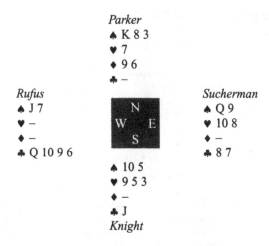

```
                        Parker
                        ♠ K 8 3
                        ♥ 7
                        ♦ 9 6
                        ♣ -
        Rufus                               Sucherman
        ♠ J 7                               ♠ Q 9
        ♥ -           N                     ♥ 10 8
        ♦ -        W     E                  ♦ -
        ♣ Q 10 9 6       S                  ♣ 8 7
                        ♠ 10 5
                        ♥ 9 5 3
                        ♦ -
                        ♣ J
                        Knight
```

When another good diamond was presented, Sucherman had no answer. If he discarded on this diamond and the next, declarer would discard his two black-suit losers and lead a trump towards the nine. If instead Sucherman ruffed high, with the 10, Knight would throw a spade. A spade return would not damage him because he could then lead the other high diamond, forcing East to ruff with his last trump; dummy's trump would then be available for a club ruff.

Sucherman eventually shrugged his shoulders and ruffed with the eight. Knight overruffed with the nine, ruffed his last club, and led the other good diamond. Whether or not East chose to ruff, he would throw his spade loser. Twelve tricks were his.

'Well done, indeed!' exclaimed Parker. He had no great opinion of Knight's play, in general, and would have been impressed had he simply cashed twelve top tricks. As for executing some sort of trump coup, this was way beyond expectations.

Sucherman, meanwhile, was not overjoyed to have picked up only five points on the first deal. Typical of his luck, whenever he played for money. At duplicate he often picked up ten points, sometimes even an opening bid or two. Was there any law that this should not happen at rubber bridge?

Sucherman sorted through his cards for the next deal, noting that he held only four points this time. Ah well, perhaps his partner, Mark Rufus, would surprise him by opening 2NT.

'Three Hearts,' said Rufus.

This was the deal:

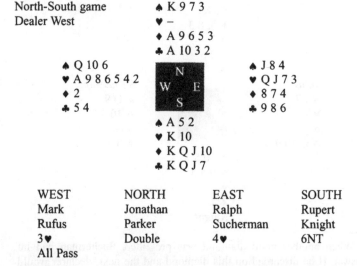

North-South game
Dealer West

♠ K 9 7 3
♥ –
♦ A 9 6 5 3
♣ A 10 3 2

♠ Q 10 6
♥ A 9 8 6 5 4 2
♦ 2
♣ 5 4

♠ J 8 4
♥ Q J 7 3
♦ 8 7 4
♣ 9 8 6

♠ A 5 2
♥ K 10
♦ K Q J 10
♣ K Q J 7

WEST	NORTH	EAST	SOUTH
Mark	Jonathan	Ralph	Rupert
Rufus	Parker	Sucherman	Knight
3♥	Double	4♥	6NT
All Pass			

Rufus led ♣5 and down went the dummy. 'My fault, Rupert,' apologised Parker. 'I may have chosen the wrong moment for a light double.'

Knight winced as he inspected the dummy. Six of a minor would have been a trivial make. If the suits broke well, he might even have made Seven Clubs, ruffing two hearts and throwing a spade on the long diamond. What could he do in 6NT? There were eleven top tricks. The only hope was to run the minors. If one of the defenders held four or more spades, he would have to reduce to just one heart. If that card was the ace, or the defender had started with the queen and jack, well, perhaps there might be a chance.

Knight cashed five rounds of diamonds, throwing a spade, then embarked on the club suit. This was the position with one club still to be played:

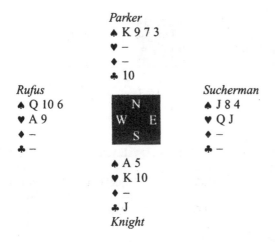

Parker
♠ K 9 7 3
♥ –
♦ –
♣ 10

Rufus
♠ Q 10 6
♥ A 9
♦ –
♣ –

Sucherman
♠ J 8 4
♥ Q J
♦ –
♣ –

♠ A 5
♥ K 10
♦ –
♣ J
Knight

When the jack of clubs appeared on the table, Rufus considered his discard carefully. Declarer was marked with the king of hearts. It was also fairly obvious to everyone, from the lack of a heart lead, that West held the ace of hearts. If he threw yet another heart, declarer would surely duck a heart to the bare ace, claiming the contract. Taking what he saw was his only chance, Rufus threw ♠6. Dummy followed suit on the last club and it was now Sucherman to play. He decided to retain his spade guard and threw ♥J.

'This is quite a hand!' exclaimed Knight. With a flourish he spun the king of hearts onto the table. West won with the ace and East's queen was pinned. Knight placed his remaining cards face-up on the table, tapping the ten of hearts with his finger. 'Twelve tricks,' he said.

Sucherman could not believe that the opponents had been dealt so many high cards. With the air of a man parting with his last photo of a loved one, he handed Knight his winnings on the rubber.

'It's worse for me,' observed Rufus, as he paid his losses to Parker.

The next rubber saw Ralph Sucherman and Rupert Knight in partnership. Sucherman, who had no great opinion of Knight's play either, steeled himself for the experience. Two-pound stakes, with such a partner? Please God that the cards would lie their way.

This was the first hand of the new rubber:

Love All   ♠ 7 3 2
Dealer South   ♥ K Q 2
                 ♦ A 9 4 3
                 ♣ K 8 3

♠ K Q J 10 5		♠ 9 6 4
♥ 9 6 5	N	♥ 10 7 4
♦ K 10 7	W E	♦ J 8 5 2
♣ 9 7	S	♣ 10 5 2

                 ♠ A 8
                 ♥ A J 8 3
                 ♦ Q 6
                 ♣ A Q J 6 4

WEST	NORTH	EAST	SOUTH
Rupert	Jonathan	Ralph	Mark
Knight	Parker	Sucherman	Rufus
–	–	–	1♣
1♠	Dble	Pass	4♥
Pass	5♣	Pass	6♣
All Pass			

Expecting his partner to hold four hearts for the negative double of West's spade overcall, Mark Rufus rebid 4♥. When Parker reverted to clubs, Rufus raised to a small slam.

Sucherman, who had been unable to hide his disgust when he picked up his one-count, beckoned for his partner to make the opening lead. Just what he had feared! The opponents in a slam and he had to defend it with this Rupert Knight opposite.

The king of spades was led and Rufus considered the matter for some moments before playing to the opening trick. If West held six spades and the king of diamonds, the contract could be made by ducking the opening lead. He would win any continuation, then cash his winners to catch West in a simple squeeze.

What if West held only five spades? It might then be better to win the first spade. East might well hold a spade higher than the eight, but this would make no difference against a moderate defender like Knight. He would surely keep the spade queen and king-one of diamonds as his last three cards. An endplay would then follow.

Rufus won the first round of spades and drew trumps in three rounds. He then proceeded to cash his winners in hearts and trumps. Contrary to expectations, Rupert Knight was alert to the risk of an endplay. He retained his precious ♠5 and the following end position was reached:

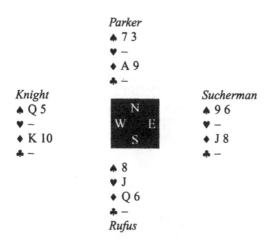

Parker
♠ 7 3
♥ –
♦ A 9
♣ –

Knight
♠ Q 5
♥ –
♦ K 10
♣ –

Sucherman
♠ 9 6
♥ –
♦ J 8
♣ –

♠ 8
♥ J
♦ Q 6
♣ –
Rufus

Rupert Knight's problems were not yet over. He had one more discard to find on declarer's last heart. Realising his fate if he threw a low spade or the guard on the diamond king, he tried the effect of throwing the queen of spades.

Rufus looked at Knight with some admiration. 'You're certainly trying your best,' he said.

Knight's best was not good enough. Rufus read the situation correctly and threw a diamond from dummy. When declarer exited with ♠8, Sucherman won with ♠9. Dummy's ♠7, along with the diamond ace, were good for the last two tricks. The slam had been made.

Sucherman glared across the table. 'King, queen, jack, ten, nine, we have between us and you let him make the seven?' he exclaimed. 'You think perhaps this is funny at two pounds a hundred?'

'No, no, he defended well,' said Rufus. 'He gets endplayed if he keeps a higher spade.'

'At least that would make you work for it,' declared Sucherman. 'This way, he hands it to you on a plate.'

'It was the right defence,' persisted Rufus. 'It would have beaten the slam if you held 9-8 of spades.'

Sucherman waved a dismissive hand. So, it is his fault for not holding the 9-8? A one-count he had been dealt, on his first money game of the cruise.

Sucherman sorted through his next hand with a look of total disbelief. Search for honour cards as he might, he could find only two tens in his hand. Because he did not express gratitude for the 1-count, he is punished with a 0-count? Oy vay! If anyone should dare to ask him to play money bridge again he would have his answer ready.

This was the deal:

```
North-South game        ♠ J 7
Dealer South            ♥ Q 8 5
                        ♦ K Q 7 5 3 2
                        ♣ K Q

        ♠ A Q 10 6 5 3      N           ♠ 8 2
        ♥ K 6 2        W        E       ♥ 10 7 4
        ♦ 4                S            ♦ 10 9 6
        ♣ A 7 4                         ♣ 9 8 6 3 2

                        ♠ K 9 4
                        ♥ A J 9 3
                        ♦ A J 8
                        ♣ J 10 5
```

WEST	NORTH	EAST	SOUTH
Rupert	Jonathan	Ralph	Mark
Knight	Parker	Sucherman	Rufus
1♠	2♦	Pass	3NT
All Pass			

Realising that he must hold nearly all of the defence's assets, Rupert Knight led the ace of spades against 3NT. Seeing a doubleton jack appear in the dummy, he was then able to continue with the queen of spades. Rufus allowed the spade queen to win and captured the third round of spades with his king. Eight tricks were visible and West could surely be end-played for a ninth.

Rufus proceeded to run the diamond suit and soon arrived at this position:

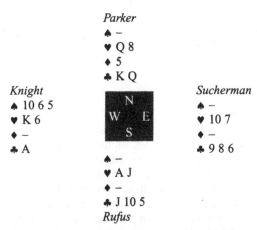

Parker
♠ –
♥ Q 8
♦ 5
♣ K Q

Knight
♠ 10 6 5
♥ K 6
♦ –
♣ A

Sucherman
♠ –
♥ 10 7
♦ –
♣ 9 8 6

♠ –
♥ A J
♦ –
♣ J 10 5
Rufus

When the last diamond was led from dummy, East and South both threw a club. Knight, who was in a similar dilemma to that of the previous hand, decided to throw ♥6.

Rufus paused to consider his next play. Where was the ♥K? West had opened the bidding and was likely to hold the missing card. Still, was a moderate player like Knight capable of baring a king? When ♥Q was led from the table, Sucherman followed with the seven. Rufus surveyed the scene uncertainly. Was a moderate player like Sucherman capable of putting him to a guess by holding off the king?

Recalling that Sucherman had sorted his cards for the deal with the air of a man walking to his own funeral, Rufus eventually placed the missing king with West. He rose with the ace, bringing down the bare king, and the third rubber was at an end.

With a sigh, Sucherman reached for his wallet. 'Can you believe this?' he said. 'During two entire rubbers my total point-count is just ten? Even for me, that is below average.'

Suddenly Mitzi Sucherman arrived on the scene. 'Such a time I have been looking for you, Ralph!' she exclaimed. 'Why did you not tell me you would be here?'

Sucherman's surreptitious attempt to return his wallet to his pocket did not escape attention. 'You are playing for money, Ralph?' Mitzi demanded. 'Against the best two players on the ship, and with Rupert as a partner, you are playing for money?'

'Fortunately the cards favoured me,' said Sucherman, rising to his feet. 'Now, let's celebrate in the bar, my dear. From my winnings I will buy you one of your favourites - Bailey's on ice!'

10
Hermann Gallus Plays Host

The *King Harald II* had docked in Sydney for a full two days and it was with some excitement that the cruisers disembarked.

'Try the mono-rail system,' Mark Rufus advised. 'Last time I was here you could buy a ticket for a one-station journey and go round the whole circuit. No-one checks your ticket while you're on the train and you eventually get off one station from where you started.'

'Thanks for the tip,' said Knight. 'I trust that you'll bail me out if I end in a Sydney jail with two butch wardresses standing over me.'

'Not me!' said Rufus. 'I wouldn't want to spoil your fun.'

Rufus's theory on the mono-rail proved to be correct and Rupert Knight spent an enjoyable day exploring the city. The following afternoon a teams-of-8 match had been arranged against the Double Bay Bridge Centre.

'I wonder if Ron Klinger will be playing!' exclaimed Mitzi Sucherman, who had a large carrier bag with her. 'I have brought all his flippers with me, so he can autograph them. Such a weight, they are. You carry them for me, Ralph.'

'You think Ron Klinger will turn up to play against players like us?' exclaimed Sucherman. 'I certainly hope not, or we will be slaughtered.'

'If he is not there, perhaps someone can phone him,' Mitzi suggested. 'He will be delighted to autograph the flippers, I am sure of it.'

The mini-bus soon arrived at the Double Bay Bridge Centre, situated in an area of pavement cafes within walking distance of the Sydney beaches. The first-floor playing rooms were airy and welcoming. Sucherman nudged his wife, indicating with an approving finger the no-smoking sign on the wall. The match was to be of 32 boards with each pair playing 8 boards against each of the opposing pairs.

The first set saw Vera Stoute and Mitzi Sucherman facing David Stern, the proprietor of the club, and Ron Greene.

Love All
Dealer West

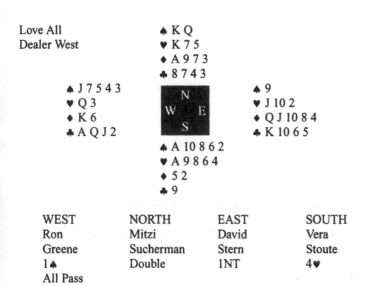

```
                        ♠ K Q
                        ♥ K 7 5
                        ♦ A 9 7 3
                        ♣ 8 7 4 3
     ♠ J 7 5 4 3                        ♠ 9
     ♥ Q 3            N                  ♥ J 10 2
     ♦ K 6        W       E              ♦ Q J 10 8 4
     ♣ A Q J 2           S              ♣ K 10 6 5
                        ♠ A 10 8 6 2
                        ♥ A 9 8 6 4
                        ♦ 5 2
                        ♣ 9
```

WEST	NORTH	EAST	SOUTH
Ron	Mitzi	David	Vera
Greene	Sucherman	Stern	Stoute
1♠	Double	1NT	4♥
All Pass			

The middle-aged West player led a spade against Four Hearts and Vera Stoute won in the dummy, noting the fall of the nine from East. What now? Should she start by drawing two rounds of trumps? No, when she set up a route to her hand, by playing on one of the minors, the defenders would be able to draw a third round of trumps. She would then be left with four losers. 'Club, please,' she said.

Ron Greene won the first round of clubs with the jack and returned another spade. When East ruffed, Mitzi raised her eyes to the ceiling. Did Vera ever remember to draw trumps? Such a moment she chooses for this aberration - just when their opponents are good players.

Vera ruffed East's club return and drew the outstanding trumps with the king and ace. She then cashed the ace of spades and led the spade 10 for a ruffing finesse. Whether or not West chose to cover with the jack, ten tricks were hers.

'Yes, clever play,' observed David Stern. 'If you draw two rounds of trumps first, you would go down. I refuse to ruff the second spade, grab the lead when you play a minor, and draw dummy's last trump.'

'Draw dummy's last trump, yes, that's what I was afraid of,' declared Mitzi. 'You took a nice line there, Vera.'

'No other lead is any better, Ron,' said the East player. 'If we open a route to the South hand, declarer will simply draw two rounds of trumps and set about the spades.'

Mitzi's mouth was open. Ron, this man is called? Was it possible that he was... She turned towards the West player. 'You are Ron Klinger?' she enquired.

Greene laughed. 'No,' he replied. 'I don't look like him and I certainly don't play like him, unfortunately.'

'He will be coming to the club tonight?' persisted Mitzi. 'I have read every flipper he has written.'

David Stern smiled. 'What about his full-size books?' he said. 'Have you read those too?'

Mitzi shook her head. 'You think, when I am so busy in London, I have time to read books? Flippers, I can make time for.'

'Ron's away on the Gold Coast, on one of his bridge holidays,' said Greene. 'He'll be sorry to have missed you.'

At another table, the eccentric and somewhat wild-haired Herman Gallus sat South for the Sydney team. Never one to miss the chance of applying some unknown convention, he was nevertheless a very capable cardplayer.

```
North-South game          ♠ A J 3
Dealer South              ♥ 4 3
                          ♦ A 6 5 3
                          ♣ A K 6 4

      ♠ 2                    N           ♠ K Q 10 9 8 7 5
      ♥ 9 6 5 2         W         E      ♥ 7
      ♦ K 10 8 2             S           ♦ 9 4
      ♣ J 9 7 5                          ♣ Q 10 2

                          ♠ 6 4
                          ♥ A K Q J 10 8
                          ♦ Q J 7
                          ♣ 8 3
```

WEST	NORTH	EAST	SOUTH
Sharon	Tom	Debbie	Herman
Glass	Gulman	Collier	Gallus
–	1NT	3♠	4♣
Pass	6♣	Pass	6♥
All Pass			

'Your partner's 4♣ bid?' queried Sharon, who was on lead.

'We're not a regular partnership,' replied Tom Gulman, looking as if he were glad of the fact. 'You'd better ask him what it means. I took the bid as natural.'

'Oh dear, oh dear,' Herman Gallus exclaimed. 'Surely South African

Texas is standard after three-level intervention? The bid shows hearts, of course.'

Sharon smiled politely at the South player. 'Thanks for explaining it,' she said.

'Pity you've never explained it to me,' Gulman retorted.

Sharon led her singleton spade and Gallus won in the dummy. He drew trumps in four rounds, then scratched the back of his neck, deep in thought. What chance was there of twelve tricks? If West held ♦K-x-x, it would be easy. He could concede a trick to the diamond king, leaving the safe hand on lead. Even if diamonds were not 3-3, this play would pave the way for a possible squeeze.

Sharon covered the diamond queen with the king and was allowed to win the trick. When she switched to a club, Gallus won in the dummy, then cashed the ace and jack of diamonds. The suit failed to break 3-3 and declarer cashed one more round of trumps to reach this end position:

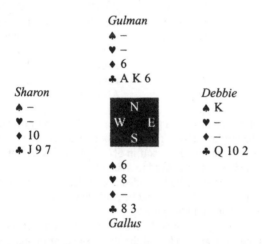

```
                    Gulman
                    ♠ —
                    ♥ —
                    ♦ 6
                    ♣ A K 6
    Sharon                          Debbie
    ♠ —                             ♠ K
    ♥ —              N              ♥ —
    ♦ 10          W     E           ♦ —
    ♣ J 9 7          S              ♣ Q 10 2
                    ♠ 6
                    ♥ 8
                    ♦ —
                    ♣ 8 3
                    Gallus
```

When Gallus led his last trump, West had to throw a club to retain his guard against dummy's last diamond. The ♦6 was thrown from dummy and East was now squeezed in the black suits. She decided to throw the spade king and declarer now scored the lowly spade six, followed by two top clubs in dummy. The slam had been made.

'Had to be in a slam,' Gallus observed. 'I had six winners in my hand, facing a strong notrump. Seven winners if you include ♠6!'

The first comparison of scores put the Sydney team in the lead by 12 IMPs. The next set of the match saw Rufus and Parker facing Dennis and Linda Wileman, winners of several national mixed pairs championships.

```
Love all                    ♠ K Q J 6 4
Dealer South                ♥ K
                            ♦ A K Q J 6
                            ♣ 9 4
        ♠ 9 8 5                           ♠ 10 7 3 2
        ♥ J 7 6 4 2        N              ♥ Q 8 5
        ♦ 10 5 2       W       E          ♦ 8 3
        ♣ A 3              S              ♣ K 8 7 5
                            ♠ A
                            ♥ A 10 9 3
                            ♦ 9 7 4
                            ♣ Q J 10 6 2
```

WEST	NORTH	EAST	SOUTH
Mark	Linda	Jonathan	Dennis
Rufus	Wileman	Parker	Wileman
–	–	–	1♣
Pass	1♠	Pass	1NT
Pass	3♦	Pass	3NT
Pass	6NT	All Pass	

Dennis Wileman added on a point or two for his good intermediates and opened the bidding. His wife was not one to hold back either and a few moments later he found himself in 6NT. West led ♠9, won in hand with the ace, and Wileman paused to assess his prospects.

It was fortunate that he had avoided a club lead. Against that, this spade lead had removed the card that he could have used to untangle his heart winners. What could be done?

Finding the ten of diamonds doubleton would not assist him. If he cashed the king of hearts and used the third round of diamonds as an entry to the heart ace, there would be no way back to dummy's spades. Wileman decided to run dummy's long suits. With one spade still to be played, both defenders were feeling the pinch in this ending:

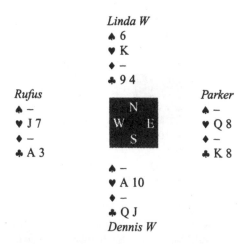

Linda W
♠ 6
♥ K
♦ —
♣ 9 4

Rufus
♠ —
♥ J 7
♦ —
♣ A 3

Parker
♠ —
♥ Q 8
♦ —
♣ K 8

♠ —
♥ A 10
♦ —
♣ Q J
Dennis W

When dummy's last spade was played, Parker threw ♣8. The next two cards on the table were the club jack from declarer and ♥7 from Rufus in the West seat. Wileman had been counting the hearts. Since there were still three out, there was no future in overtaking the heart king. He cashed the card instead, then called for a low club, the king appearing from East.

There was nothing that Rufus could do. If he allowed partner's club king to win, declarer would take the last trick with his ace of hearts. If instead he overtook with the club ace, dummy's ♣9 would score.

As soon as West had thought for a second or two, it was clear how the cards lay. 'Twelve tricks?' said Wileman, facing his last card - the heart ace.

'Yep,' Rufus replied. 'I needed to lead a club. I was never going to find that.'

'The spade lead caused me quite a problem, actually,' Wileman observed. 'Lead a red suit and I have twelve tricks on top.'

On a nearby table, it was Sucherman and Knight's turn to face Herman Gallus. This players drew their cards for this board:

Love all   ♠ A K 8 3
Dealer West   ♥ 10 9 4
                ♦ 6 4 2
                ♣ Q 8 2

♠ Q J 2		♠ 9 7 4
♥ A K J 3 2	N	♥ Q 8 7 5
♦ K 7 3	W E	♦ 10 9 8 5
♣ 4 3	S	♣ J 6

                ♠ 10 6 5
                ♥ 6
                ♦ A Q J
                ♣ A K 10 9 7 5

WEST	NORTH	EAST	SOUTH
Rupert	Tom	Ralph	Herman
Knight	Gulman	Sucherman	Gallus
1♥	Pass	Pass	3♣
Pass	Pass	3♥	Dble
Pass	4♥	Pass	5♣
All Pass			

Ralph Sucherman was somewhat perturbed when his protective bid of 3♥ led to the opponents reaching game. He turned towards the North player. 'You tell me this 3♣ is weak?' he demanded. 'After a weak bid, he can double to contest further?'

Herman Gallus smiled at this. 'My partner is not exactly the world's leading expert on the system we're playing,' he replied. 'Jumps are intermediate in fourth seat, of course.'

Sucherman spread his hands. 'In that case we have been damaged,' he said. 'I would not have bid again.'

Gulman proffered his convention card. 'It says weak here,' he said. 'The bid was wrong, I'm afraid, not the explanation.'

Herman Gallus grabbed his partner's convention card and scribbled a change onto it, proceeding to alter his own card too. 'Not even a one-legged Kiwi would play weak in fourth,' he said.

Rupert Knight led the king of hearts against Five Clubs. Gallus ruffed the heart continuation and drew one round of trumps with the ace. He then overtook ♣9 with the queen, both defenders following. After ruffing dummy's last heart, he cashed dummy's two top spades. These cards remained:

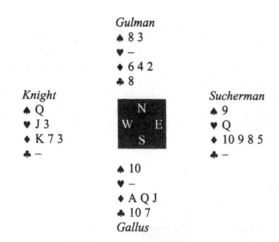

Gulman
♠ 8 3
♥ –
♦ 6 4 2
♣ 8

Knight
♠ Q
♥ J 3
♦ K 7 3
♣ –

Sucherman
♠ 9
♥ Q
♦ 10 9 8 5
♣ –

♠ 10
♥ –
♦ A Q J
♣ 10 7
Gallus

A spade exit to the queen left West with no good card to play. A heart would allow declarer to ruff in the dummy and discard one diamond loser from his hand. The other diamond loser could then be thrown on the thirteenth spade. Knight tried a diamond instead, but declarer won with the jack. Thanks to his earlier unblock in the trump suit, he was then able to cross to dummy's ♣8 and discard the diamond queen on the thirteenth spade. The game had been made.

Sucherman sought to stall any complaints about his re-opening of the auction. 'What a defence you play here!' he exclaimed. 'You could not unblock the spade honours, in case I hold the 10?'

'I might have done,' replied Knight. 'He had the 10 anyway. It didn't make any difference.'

Sucherman was not to be placated. 'The ace of hearts, you lead at Trick 1,' he continued. 'After my 3♥ bid, you could not lead a low heart? I win with the queen and put a diamond through!'

Knight blinked. 'That would work, as it happens,' he replied. 'It's absolutely double-dummy, though. Why should I risk it?'

Gallus laughed at this. 'Wouldn't beat it, anyway,' he declared. 'You had the ace-king-jack of hearts, didn't you? You'd be squeezed in the majors.'

'Exactly,' said Knight, grateful for the reprieve.

'It was good contract,' Gallus continued. 'We might have bid it more smoothly, I suppose.'

A supper was to be served later and at half-time the players took a few sandwiches and a quick cup of coffee (the club's cappuccinos were famous and attracted players from miles away).

'Not much taste in these egg sandwiches,' observed Gallus loudly. 'A touch of Vegemite would liven them up. You don't have any, I suppose?'

Linda Wileman sent a withering glance in Gallus's direction. 'I'll leave the making of the sandwiches to you next time,' she replied. 'You might find some Vegemite in the kitchen.'

'Just an observation,' Gallus continued. 'Not worth trudging all the way to the kitchen, anyway. These cheese ones are quite edible.'

The second half started with Rufus and Parker facing Margi Troke and Lydia Malcolm.

```
Love all                    ♠ 2
Dealer South                ♥ A 6 4
                            ♦ A K J 10 7 6
                            ♣ 8 3 2
        ♠ A Q 10 8 7                          ♠ 9 4 3
        ♥ 8 5 3             N                 ♥ K 2
        ♦ 5 3           W       E             ♦ Q 9 8 2
        ♣ Q 10 6            S                 ♣ J 9 5 4
                            ♠ K J 6 5
                            ♥ Q J 10 9 7
                            ♦ 4
                            ♣ A K 7
```

WEST	NORTH	EAST	SOUTH
Margi	Jonathan	Lydia	Mark
Troke	Parker	Malcolm	Rufus
–	–	–	1♥
1♠	2♦	2♠	Pass
Pass	4♥	All Pass	

Troke led a trump against the heart game, her partner winning with the king and returning a second round of trumps. Rufus won in hand with the queen. What now?

If he took a straightforward diamond finesse and it lost, East would play a spade through and two rounds of the suit would force dummy's ace of trumps. He would then need two more rounds of diamonds to stand up. Perhaps it would be better to take a ruffing finesse in diamonds, into the safe hand.

Rufus crossed to the ace of diamonds and led the diamond jack. If East had covered, declarer would have ruffed and drawn the remaining trump, enjoying the whole diamond suit. Sensing this, Lydia Malcolm declined to cover. Declarer threw a club and the jack of diamonds won the trick. Rufus now drew the last trump with dummy's ace and continued with the king of diamonds, throwing one of his spade losers. West showed out on this trick, leaving these cards still to be played:

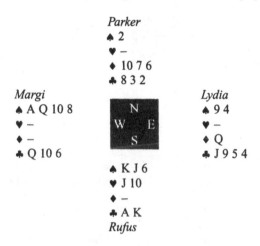

Parker
♠ 2
♥ –
♦ 10 7 6
♣ 8 3 2

Margi
♠ A Q 10 8
♥ –
♦ –
♣ Q 10 6

Lydia
♠ 9 4
♥ –
♦ Q
♣ J 9 5 4

♠ K J 6
♥ J 10
♦ –
♣ A K
Rufus

Rufus ruffed a diamond in his hand, West throwing a spade. He then cashed his last trump. Margi Troke spent some time considering what to throw. There was no good answer, in fact. If she threw a spade, declarer would be able to duck two spades, setting up his king for a tenth trick. She chose instead to throw a club. Rufus now cashed the two top clubs and exited with the king of spades. West had to win with the ace and, at Trick 12, lead from the spade queen. The game had been made.

The two women shared a quick glance. Was there anything they could have done about it? It seemed not.

Meanwhile, it was the turn of Vera Stoute and Mitzi Sucherman to face the eccentric Herman Gallus and his partner.

'Here's a blast from the past,' declared Gallus, who was inspecting the opponents' convention card. 'They're playing a double raise in a major as a straightforward limit bid!'

Vera Stoute glared at the wild-haired Australian. 'It shows about 10 points,' she said. 'Isn't that normal?'

'Over here we all play modified Bergen raises,' Gallus replied. 'The sequence 1♠ - 3♠ shows 0-6 points and four-card support.'

Tom Gulman gave a small sigh. 'Now he tells me,' he said.

The players drew their cards for this board:

East-West game
Dealer South

♠ A 10 9 6
♥ A 8 7
♦ 10 8 6 3 2
♣ A

♠ 3
♥ Q 10 6 5
♦ K Q J 4
♣ 10 8 7 2

N
W E
S

♠ J 7 5 2
♥ K J 9 4 3
♦ 9 7
♣ J 5

♠ K Q 8 4
♥ 2
♦ A 5
♣ K Q 9 6 4 3

WEST	NORTH	EAST	SOUTH
Vera	Herman	Mitzi	Tom
Stoute	Gallus	Sucherman	Gulman
–	–	–	1♣
Pass	1♦	Pass	1♠
Pass	4♣	Pass	6♣
Pass	6♠	All Pass	

Vera Stoute led the king of diamonds and Gallus displayed his dummy. 'I knew you'd got it wrong when you didn't alert my 4♣,' he informed his partner. 'I play that as a splinter bid agreeing spades.'

Gulman surveyed his partner wearily. 'I'm supposed to know that, somehow?' he said.

'I thought everyone played it that way,' Gallus replied. 'To agree clubs I would jump in the fourth suit.'

'Ah yes, of course,' said Gulman. Why on earth had he agreed to play with this madman? He certainly wouldn't rush to repeat the experience.

Gulman won the diamond lead in his hand and turned his mind to countering any bad breaks in the black suits. If the club suit was 4-2 and needed to be ruffed good, it seemed he could deal with a 4-1 trump break only if East had the long trumps. Yes, and with the diamond ace already gone he must be careful to avoid a blockage in the trump suit.

Gulman crossed to the ace of clubs at Trick 2, then led the 10 of trumps to his king. His next move was to ruff a club with dummy's nine. West showed out when the ace of trumps was played but, after the double unblock, the way was clear to lead the spade six to declarer's eight. Gulman drew the last trump with the queen and claimed twelve tricks.

'That doesn't look very good for us,' said Vera Stoute. 'They only had 26 points. I don't suppose they would have got there without the bidding misunderstanding.'

Gallus let out a loud cackle of laughter, drawing disapproving glances from around the room. 'My partner only had four losers in his hand,' he said. 'More likely to get to a grand than to stop in game!'

The final set was well under way when a potential slam hand arrived at Rupert Knight's table.

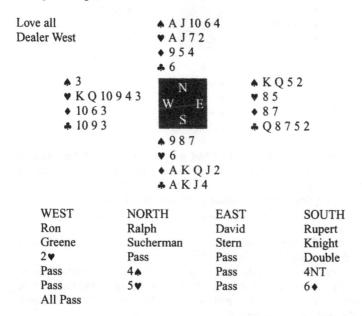

Love all
Dealer West

North: ♠ A J 10 6 4 ♥ A J 7 2 ♦ 9 5 4 ♣ 6

West: ♠ 3 ♥ K Q 10 9 4 3 ♦ 10 6 3 ♣ 10 9 3

East: ♠ K Q 5 2 ♥ 8 5 ♦ 8 7 ♣ Q 8 7 5 2

South: ♠ 9 8 7 ♥ 6 ♦ A K Q J 2 ♣ A K J 4

WEST	NORTH	EAST	SOUTH
Ron	Ralph	David	Rupert
Greene	Sucherman	Stern	Knight
2♥	Pass	Pass	Double
Pass	4♠	Pass	4NT
Pass	5♥	Pass	6♦
All Pass			

Greene decided to lead his singleton spade and down went the dummy.

'I'm glad you said diamonds and not clubs,' observed Sucherman as he laid out the dummy. 'My hand would be useless for clubs.'

Knight nodded his thanks for the dummy. It wasn't that obvious how useful the dummy would be for diamonds. The lead was surely a singleton and in that case, how could he avoid two spade losers? Suddenly inspiration struck. Perhaps there was a chance! 'Ace, please,' he said.

At Trick 2 Knight took a successful finesse of the jack of clubs. A club ruff was followed by five rounds of trumps and the two top clubs. This position remained:

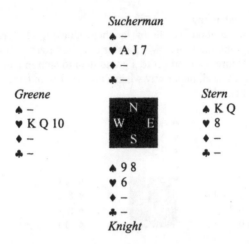

Sucherman
♠ –
♥ A J 7
♦ –
♣ –

Greene
♠ –
♥ K Q 10
♦ –
♣ –

Stern
♠ K Q
♥ 8
♦ –
♣ –

♠ 9 8
♥ 6
♦ –
♣ –
Knight

When a heart was led, West had no counter. He tried the effect of inserting the queen, but Knight called for dummy's seven. West had to give dummy the last two tricks and the slam had been made.

'Such a play you make there!' congratulated Sucherman.

A somewhat dazed Rupert Knight smiled back at him. 'It wasn't bad, was it?' he said.

'King of hearts lead works better,' observed David Stern. 'Still, I can see the singleton looked a better bet.'

'I think he can still do it, even if I lead the king of hearts,' Greene replied. 'He wins with the ace, then plays ace of clubs, ruff a club, trump, ruff a club. He then ruffs a heart in his hand and draws trumps. What cards does that leave?'

Greene reached for his score-card and scribbled this diagram on the back:

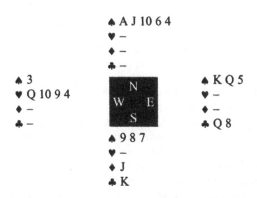

```
                        ♠ A J 10 6 4
                        ♥ —
                        ♦ —
                        ♣ —
    ♠ 3                      N           ♠ K Q 5
    ♥ Q 10 9 4           W       E       ♥ —
    ♦ —                      S           ♦ —
    ♣ —                                  ♣ Q 8
                        ♠ 9 8 7
                        ♥ —
                        ♦ J
                        ♣ K
```

'On the last trump, you have to throw a club, David,' continued Greene. 'Otherwise he can duck a spade and set up the suit. Declarer cashes the ace of clubs and endplays you with a spade!'

Knight blinked as he tried to understand what the Australian was saying. 'That's the line I had in mind,' he declared, nodding learnedly. 'Did you follow that, Ralph?'

Meanwhile, it was the girls' turn to deal with Herman Gallus.

```
North-South game       ♠ J 10 3 2
Dealer South           ♥ A Q 5
                       ♦ A Q 4
                       ♣ 9 6 3
    ♠ —                     N          ♠ 9 8 6 4
    ♥ 10 9 8 2          W       E      ♥ K J 7 4 3
    ♦ J 9 8 3               S          ♦ 10 5
    ♣ K J 10 8 2                       ♣ Q 7
                       ♠ A K Q 7 5
                       ♥ 6
                       ♦ K 7 6 2
                       ♣ A 5 4
```

WEST	NORTH	EAST	SOUTH
Sharon	Tom	Debbie	Herman
Glass	Gulman	Collier	Gallus
–	–	–	1♠
Pass	4♠	Pass	5♦
Pass	5♠	Pass	5NT
Pass	6♠	All Pass	

'You alerted the 5♠ bid?' queried Sharon, who was on lead.

'Yes,' replied Gallus. 'My 5♦ was a New South Wales long-suit slam try and the two-step response showed second-round control.'

Tom Gulman, who could barely suppress his amusement, leaned forward. 'Are you completely mad?' he demanded. 'I've never even heard of such a method. I took your 5♦ as a cue-bid, of course.'

'And the 5NT bid?' continued Sharon.

'I hadn't the faintest idea what it meant,' said Gulman. 'Since he'd only opened at the one-level, I intended my 6♠ as a sign-off.'

'The 5NT was a cost-nothing pick-a-slam bid,' declared Gallus. 'Just in case you'd bid 4♠ with a long side suit in one of the minors. If you stop and think about it, I don't see what else it can mean.'

Sharon led ♥10 and down went the dummy. Gallus considered his options. Was it possible that the girl had led from a K-10-9 holding? No, women tended to choose safe leads. In any case there were fair chances, even if ♥K was offside. 'Play the ace,' he instructed.

The line Gallus had in mind was a dummy reversal, combined with a minor-suit squeeze if the diamonds did not break. He ruffed a heart with a low trump, then ducked a club. East overtook West's ♣10 with the queen and played a second club. Gallus won with the ace and crossed to dummy with the jack of trumps, West showing out. His next move was to ruff dummy's ♥Q with the ace. The king and queen of trumps came next and Gallus then crossed to dummy with a top diamond. This was the position as East's last trump was drawn:

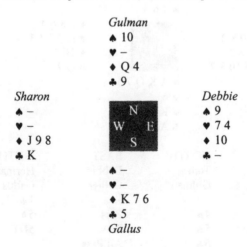

Gulman
♠ 10
♥ –
♦ Q 4
♣ 9

Sharon
♠ –
♥ –
♦ J 9 8
♣ K

Debbie
♠ 9
♥ 7 4
♦ 10
♣ –

Gallus
♠ –
♥ –
♦ K 7 6
♣ 5

Gallus threw ♣5 from his hand and Sharon had no good discard. Knowing that she had to keep a guard on dummy's ♣9, she threw a diamond. 'I expect these diamonds are good,' declared Gallus, facing his remaining cards.

The two girls nodded resignedly and the slam had been made.

'Not so easy to get there without the New South Wales method,' Gallus declared. 'I didn't have much of a hand.'

The Sydney team had won the match by a healthy 42 IMPs and the players moved to a side room where a splendid light supper was to be served. Debbie and Sharon took two adjacent seats but Herman Gallus arrived with a spare chair and wedged himself between them. 'You pretty young things been to Oz before?' he asked.

'No, it's the first time,' Debbie replied.

'I don't suppose you've eaten proper prawns before, in that case,' Gallus continued. 'You won't believe the taste of these beauties. Tom! Do something useful for a change. Pass over those prawns, will you?'

11
Marilyn Platt's Four Doubles

The main pairs championship of the Far East section of the cruise was to take place over two consecutive evenings. Rupert Knight had been coerced into partnering a glamorous 50-year-old, Marilyn Platt. She had played in few of the other bridge sessions and Knight had no great hopes of doing at all well. Rather to his surprise, his new partner turned out to be a sensible bidder and a more than competent cardplayer.

The second session of the championship was only five minutes away as Knight found himself admiring this leader board:

1.	Marilyn Platt and Rupert Knight	64.1%
2.	Mark Rufus and Jonathan Parker	59.6%
3.	Felicity and Giles Couttes-Browne	58.2%
4.	Debbie Collier and Sharon Glass	57.6%

Suddenly he was aware of a powerful musk-based perfume in the air and felt a warm arm slip round his waist. 'Sixty-four percent!' exclaimed Marilyn Platt. 'I'll be so excited if we manage to win.'

Knight was quick to dampen her expectations. 'We're only one top ahead,' he replied. 'Not much of a lead with Rufus and Parker breathing down your necks.'

Marilyn laughed. 'Don't be silly, Rupert!' she replied. 'You're the bridge expert, aren't you? We can't let a couple of young men overtake us. I won't allow it to happen.'

The first round of the second session saw Knight and his partner facing the Suchermans.

East-West game
Dealer South

		♠ 8 7 6	
		♥ A 3	
		♦ A K 7 6 3	
		♣ Q 8 6	

♠ J 4 2		♠ 10 3
♥ 8	N	♥ J 10 9 7 6 2
♦ Q J 10 9 4 2	W E	♦ –
♣ J 9 2	S	♣ A 10 5 4 3

		♠ A K Q 9 5	
		♥ K Q 5 4	
		♦ 8 5	
		♣ K 7	

WEST	NORTH	EAST	SOUTH
Mitzi	Marilyn	Ralph	Rupert
Sucherman	Platt	Sucherman	Knight
–	–	–	1♠
Pass	2♦	Pass	2♥
Pass	4♠	Pass	4NT
Pass	5♥	Pass	6♠
Pass	Pass	Dble	6NT
All Pass			

When Knight and his partner came to a halt in 6♠, Sucherman made a Lightner Double to a lead of dummy's first-bid suit, diamonds. Knight removed to 6NT, to prevent the opponents from scoring the threatened ruff, and there was no further bidding.

The queen of diamonds was led and Knight won in the dummy, East showing out as expected. What were the prospects? If the spade suit divided 3-2, as it would have to, there would be ten top tricks. An eleventh could be established in the club suit but the source of a twelfth was harder to spot. It was barely possible for East to hold a doubleton ace of clubs. A better chance was that he should hold the ace of clubs and the heart guard as well. Yes, he would play for that chance. 'Small club, please,' said Knight.

East played low on the first round of clubs and the king won the trick. Knight now played on spades, pleased to see the suit divide 3-2. When all five spades had been played, this was the position:

Marilyn
♠ –
♥ A 3
♦ K 7
♣ Q 8

Mitzi
♠ –
♥ 8
♦ J 10 9
♣ J 9

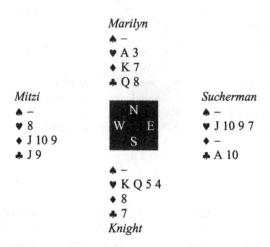

Sucherman
♠ –
♥ J 10 9 7
♦ –
♣ A 10

♠ –
♥ K Q 5 4
♦ 8
♣ 7

Knight

A diamond to the king put Sucherman to an awkward discard. Since South had bid hearts, he decided to retain his holding in that suit, bearing the ace of clubs instead.

When ♣10 appeared on the table, Knight had no difficulty in reading the lie of the cards. If East had started with A-J-10 to six clubs, he would surely have inserted the jack or ten on the first round of the suit. He must therefore have started with six hearts and five clubs to the A-10. 'Eight of clubs, please,' he said.

Somewhat reluctantly, Sucherman produced the ace of clubs. Knight could now claim the remaining tricks.

'They would have gone down in Six Spades!' exclaimed Mitzi Sucherman. 'What a foolish double you make there, Ralph. You think I need a Lightner Double to persuade me to lead a diamond?'

'A void in dummy's suit and an ace, I hold,' declared Sucherman. 'I have never seen a more obvious double. Without the double you would let it through by leading your singleton heart.'

'With queen-jack-ten to six diamonds, I would lead a singleton heart?' said Mitzi. 'Don't make me laugh.'

'A heart lead beats Six Spades too, doesn't it?' said Knight. 'What can I do with the fourth heart? I can't ruff it because West is shorter in the suit than the dummy.'

'Quite right,' continued Mitzi. 'Pass them out in Six Spades and they go down whatever I lead.'

It seemed to Rupert Knight that a heart lead would have beaten 6NT too, killing a vital entry. In the ending that had arisen, he needed a heart entry to both his own hand and the dummy.

A round or two later, Knight and his partner faced the Couttes-Brownes. The Surrey pair reached a slam on this board:

```
Love All                    ♠ K Q J 7 2
Dealer South                ♥ Q J 6
                            ♦ Q J 4
                            ♣ 8 6
        ♠ 9 8 6 5         ┌─────────┐        ♠ 4
        ♥ 10 9 3          │    N    │        ♥ 8 7 4 2
        ♦ 10 8 2          │  W   E  │        ♦ K 7 6 3
        ♣ K J 2           │    S    │        ♣ 10 9 7 4
                          └─────────┘
                            ♠ A 10 3
                            ♥ A K 5
                            ♦ A 9 5
                            ♣ A Q 5 3
```

WEST	NORTH	EAST	SOUTH
Marilyn	Felicity	Rupert	Giles
Platt	C-Brown	Knight	C-Brown
–	–	–	2NT
Pass	3♥	Pass	4♠
Pass	4NT	Pass	5♦
Pass	6♠	End	

With little justification, Giles Couttes-Browne broke his partner's transfer response, rebidding 4♠ instead of 3♠. When Marilyn led ♥10 against the resultant slam, he won with the ace and drew trumps in four rounds. 'Queen of diamonds, please,' he said.

Knight declined to cover, dummy's queen winning the trick. Couttes-Browne studied his remaining assets. What next? All would be well if the king of clubs was onside. What chance was there if West held that card?

Spotting an extra chance, Couttes-Browne called for dummy's jack of diamonds, covered by the king and ace. He then cashed his two other heart winners, leaving this end position:

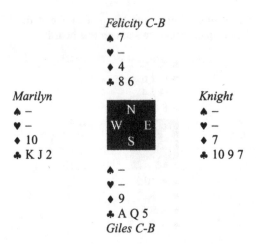

Felicity C-B
♠ 7
♥ –
♦ 4
♣ 8 6

Marilyn
♠ –
♥ –
♦ 10
♣ K J 2

Knight
♠ –
♥ –
♦ 7
♣ 10 9 7

♠ –
♥ –
♦ 9
♣ A Q 5
Giles C-B

Couttes-Browne now exited with ♦9. There was no risk attached to this play. If one of the defenders held ♦10 7 and was able to exit safely with the last diamond, declarer could ruff in the dummy and still take the club finesse. As it was, Marilyn had to win with the bare 10. She was forced to return a club into the tenace and the slam was made.

'Brilliant play, Giles!' exclaimed Felicity Couttes-Browne, peering down her considerable nose. 'Not many people would make that one, with the club finesse wrong.'

Knight steeled himself to accept the bottom graciously. Brilliant play, she calls it. Since when did a totally obvious endplay qualify in that category?

'Yes, it's a joint top,' Felicity continued, entering the score with somewhat of a flourish. 'Two pairs didn't even bid a slam! I can't believe that when I held twelve points opposite a 2NT opening.'

With some difficulty Knight managed to maintain his bridge organiser's smile. It was amazing what a wide variety of people had booked on this cruise. Most of them were as pleasant as you could wish to meet. Others - no names mentioned - were totally obnoxious. With any luck, Giles would misplay the next hand and they could emerge from the round with no great damage to their score.

This was the next board:

Game All   ♠ A Q 5 2
Dealer East   ♥ 9 7 6
            ♦ A 5
            ♣ K J 7 2

♠ K 7   ♠ J 10 6
♥ A 10 8 3   ♥ Q J 4
♦ Q J 8   ♦ 10 9 6 4 2
♣ 10 8 6 5   ♣ 9 3

            ♠ 9 8 4 3
            ♥ K 5 2
            ♦ K 7 3
            ♣ A Q 4

WEST	NORTH	EAST	SOUTH
Marilyn	Felicity	Rupert	Giles
Platt	C-Brown	Knight	C-Brown
–	–	Pass	1NT
Pass	2♣	Pass	2♠
Pass	4♠	End	

Marilyn led ♦Q and down went the dummy. 'Fourteen points for you,' observed Felicity. 'Even the weaker pairs should be in game on this one.'

Giles Couttes-Browne won the opening lead with the diamond king and took a successful finesse in trumps. When he cashed the ace of trumps, the king fell on his left. He now needed to discard a heart loser on the fourth club.

Declarer tried his luck in the club suit but Knight was able to ruff the third round. A switch to the queen of hearts gave the defenders three tricks in that suit and the game was one down.

'Nothing wrong with the contract,' declared Couttes-Browne. 'I needed Rupert to have at least three clubs. Or to hold the ace of hearts, of course.'

'We'll just have to hope that some other pairs bid game,' said Felicity sourly. 'Anyone stopping in a part-score will get an undeserved top, of course.'

Marilyn Platt turned towards the declarer. 'I was wondering if you could have made it,' she said. 'You had quite a strong dummy.'

Couttes-Browne blinked. This Marilyn character might be an expert in dressing up mutton as lamb. That hardly qualified her to lecture him on cardplay, did it?

Rupert Knight leaned forward. 'Marilyn's quite right, actually,' he said. 'You should lead the second round of trumps from your hand. You can duck, then, when the king appears. I wouldn't gain the lead to play a heart through.'

Felicity Couttes-Browne looked severely at her husband. 'Is that right, Giles?' she said.

'I never go over hands, once they're finished,' her husband replied. 'Anyone can make clever remarks once they know how the cards lie.'

'The technique is known as Avoidance Play, Giles,' continued Knight. 'It's my fault for not mentioning it in one of my talks.'

The tension was maintained on the next round when Knight and his partner faced Rufus and Parker, their main challengers. This was the first board:

```
Love All              ♠ Q 7 4
Dealer South          ♥ Q 10 9 4
                      ♦ K 9 4
                      ♣ 9 4 2
      ♠ 8 5 2                          ♠ A 10 9 6 3
      ♥ J 8 7 5 3         N            ♥ A 2
      ♦ Q 10 7        W       E        ♦ J 8 2
      ♣ J 8               S            ♣ Q 10 7
                      ♠ K J
                      ♥ K 6
                      ♦ A 6 5 3
                      ♣ A K 6 5 3
```

WEST	NORTH	EAST	SOUTH
Marilyn	Mark	Rupert	Jonathan
Platt	Rufus	Knight	Parker
–	–	–	1♣
Pass	1♥	1♠	2NT
Pass	3NT	End	

Parker ended in 3NT and Marilyn led ♠5. Knight inserted the nine and, after a few moments thought, Parker won with the king rather than the jack.

Playing on clubs first would give him only eight tricks, so Parker's next move was to lead the king of hearts. Knight had to win, or declarer would pocket the heart trick and revert to clubs. When he returned a low spade, declarer followed with the jack and West played the eight to indicate an original three-card holding. 'Queen, please,' said Parker.

With the defensive communications intact, there was no future in playing on clubs. Instead Parker exited with dummy's remaining spade. Knight won with the ace and cashed two more rounds of the suit, his partner throwing a heart and a club. These cards remained:

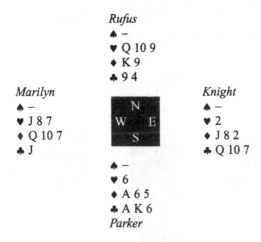

Rufus
♠ –
♥ Q 10 9
♦ K 9
♣ 9 4

Marilyn
♠ –
♥ J 8 7
♦ Q 10 7
♣ J

Knight
♠ –
♥ 2
♦ J 8 2
♣ Q 10 7

Parker
♠ –
♥ 6
♦ A 6 5
♣ A K 6

When Knight exited with a club, Parker rose with the ace and cashed a second round of clubs. The suit failed to divide, but West had to release her ♦7. Parker finessed ♥10 successfully and cashed the heart queen. This suit, too, failed to divide but Knight was caught in a minor-suit squeeze. He decided to keep his guard on clubs, the suit that South had bid. When Parker saw a further diamond discard, he read the position correctly, throwing his ♣6. He scored the last three tricks in diamonds and the game had been made.

'That was good!' congratulated Rufus. 'You needed to win the first trick with the king, didn't you? You can't exit in spades otherwise.'

'I think so,' Parker replied.

Knight was less enthusiastic about the board. 'Is it better if I don't cash my spades?' he asked.

'What did you have in clubs?' asked Parker. 'I'd need to be able to duck a club to your partner in that case.'

Parker surveyed the East curtain card. 'No, I still make it,' he said. 'If you play the seven on the first round of clubs, I can duck to West's eight. If you play the ten instead, I can win, go back to dummy and lead a second round. You can't afford to put the queen in or dummy's nine would become good.

Marilyn scored above average on the next board, making a diamond part-score. Knight met her eyes as the change of round was called and the dreaded duo departed. Yes! They had survived the two most important boards of the session. They would now have every chance of winning the event.

Next to arrive was the American, Oakley Hampton. It had been difficult to find him a partner for two consecutive sessions and a retired doctor, George Bales, had been pressed into service. This was the first board of the round:

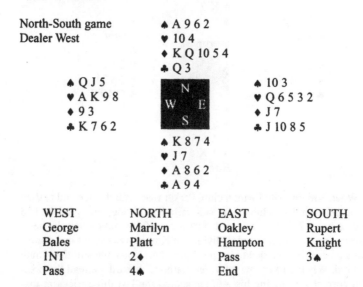

```
North-South game        ♠ A 9 6 2
Dealer West             ♥ 10 4
                        ♦ K Q 10 5 4
                        ♣ Q 3
        ♠ Q J 5              N          ♠ 10 3
        ♥ A K 9 8        W       E      ♥ Q 6 5 3 2
        ♦ 9 3               S          ♦ J 7
        ♣ K 7 6 2                       ♣ J 10 8 5
                        ♠ K 8 7 4
                        ♥ J 7
                        ♦ A 8 6 2
                        ♣ A 9 4
```

WEST	NORTH	EAST	SOUTH
George	Marilyn	Oakley	Rupert
Bales	Platt	Hampton	Knight
1NT	2♦	Pass	3♠
Pass	4♠	End	

West opened with a weak notrump and Marilyn entered the auction with an Astro 2♦ overcall, showing spades and another suit. Since she had been known to make such bids on eight points or so, Knight bid only 3♠ in response. Marilyn raised him to game and the ace of hearts was led.

'Only eleven points for you, Rupert,' said Marilyn, laying out the dummy as attractively as she could. 'I do have a useful five-timer for you in diamonds.'

'Thank you, Marilyn,' Knight replied. It was amazing that she overbid so much. Many of his partners during the cruise felt uncomfortable straying beyond a part-score.

Oakley Hampton contributed the six of hearts to the first trick and Knight followed with the jack. George Bales continued with the heart king at Trick 2, then switched to ♦9. Knight won with dummy's king and cashed two rounds of trumps, pleased to see the suit breaking 3-2.

His next move was to run the diamond suit.

Realising that he would be endplayed if he ruffed, West discarded one heart and two clubs. This brought him only temporary relief. Knight exited with a trump to West's queen and he then had to surrender the game-going trick. A club would allow dummy's queen to score; a heart would give a ruff-and-discard.

'I thought game would be there,' observed Marilyn Platt, reaching for her score-card. 'Some people say you shouldn't count two points for queen doubleton, but that's silly in my opinion.'

'We do better if I underlead my king of hearts at Trick 2,' said George Bales. 'You can win with the queen and clear a club trick for me.'

'That's how we would have defended in our game back in Minnesota,' Hampton replied. 'Didn't you see my come-on signal with the six?'

'I only play the seven or higher as a come-on,' Bales declared. 'In any case, declarer followed with the jack on the first round. If he had another heart, I thought it would be the queen.'

The last round of the session brought Debbie and Sharon to Knight's table. Knight gathered his concentration. Two more good boards and he and Marilyn would surely have an excellent chance of winning. They hadn't done particularly well against Rufus and Parker, it was true, but they did have a fair lead from the first session.

Marilyn looked somewhat concerned as the younger females took their seats. Rupert Knight had a roving eye, she had noticed, and the two girls were wearing unusually low-cut dresses. Let's hope that he could maintain his concentration for just one more round.

Marilyn scored well herself on the first board, making a spade game that had proved too difficult elsewhere. This was the last board of the event:

East-West game
Dealer South

♠ J 7 5 3 2
♥ 8 6 3
♦ 10 5 4
♣ K 4

	♠ –	N	♠ 10 8 4
	♥ K Q 9 7 4 2	W E	♥ J
	♦ A K Q 3	S	♦ 9 8 6 2
	♣ J 9 5		♣ Q 10 7 6 3

♠ A K Q 9 6
♥ A 10 5
♦ J 7
♣ A 8 2

WEST	NORTH	EAST	SOUTH
Debbie	Marilyn	Sharon	Rupert
Collier	Platt	Glass	Knight
–	–	–	1♠
2♥	2♠	Pass	4♠
All Pass			

Debbie led ♦A against the spade game, continuing with the king and queen of the suit. Knight ruffed the third round and drew trumps in three rounds. He cashed the king and ace of clubs and ruffed his last club in dummy. These cards remained:

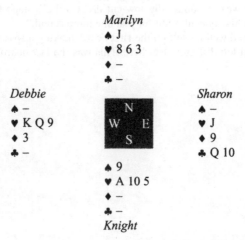

Marilyn
♠ J
♥ 8 6 3
♦ –
♣ –

Debbie
♠ –
♥ K Q 9
♦ 3
♣ –

Sharon
♠ –
♥ J
♦ 9
♣ Q 10

♠ 9
♥ A 10 5
♦ –
♣ –
Knight

When Knight called for a heart from dummy, the jack appeared on his right. This was just what he had been hoping for. He played low from his own hand and the defenders were left without resource. If Debbie overtook, she would have to lead back into declarer's A-10 tenace, or concede a ruff-and-discard. She actually chose to follow with the nine, leaving Sharon on lead. When Sharon exited with a club, Knight ruffed in the South hand and discarded a heart from dummy. The remaining tricks were his.

'Excellent, Rupert!' congratulated Marilyn. Good boards were always welcome, but good boards against this particular opposition, at such a stage of the event, were doubly welcome.

'Nothing I could do,' said Sharon. 'He was out of both minors.'

'Could we have beaten it?' asked Debbie.

It seemed to Knight that a heart switch at Trick 3, either the king or a low heart, would have broken the end-play. Defenders playing the 'king for count, ace for attitude' method of opening leads would have led the king of diamonds, requesting a count signal. When East suggested four cards in the suit, there would be every reason to switch to the king of hearts. Playing against the Couttes-Brownes, he would have pointed this out.

Knight gazed into Debbie's pale blue eyes. 'You did all you could,' he replied. 'You can't beat it, if I take that line.'

Knight was fairly sure that he and Marilyn had done enough to win the event. Humming happily to himself, he entered the results from the travelling score-sheet into his personal computer. Sure enough, these were the leading positions that appeared on the screen.

1.	Marilyn Platt and Rupert Knight	62.9%
2.	Mark Rufus and Jonathan Parker	61.3%
3.	Mitzi and Ralph Sucherman	57.3%
4.	Debbie Collier and Sharon Glass	56.0%

Incredible! Over two full sessions, and playing with a punter, he had managed to finish ahead of Rufus and Parker.

Knight printed down several copies of the result sheet and posted them prominently around the ship. Not long afterwards, Marilyn was gratefully plying him with drinks in the Captain's Lookout bar. 'Whisky always makes me feel woozy,' she said, placing a hand on Knight's knee. 'Two or three doubles and I'm anyone's.'

Knight placed his own hand on top of hers, to prevent it from advancing any further. He had seen her consume at least four doubles and they didn't stint on the measures on cruise ships like this.

Marilyn leant towards him, nuzzling ever closer. Once more he was aware of her musky perfume. He looked around the bar to see if anyone was watching them.

'I'd better not have any more to drink,' declared Marilyn, rising unsteadily to her feet. She peered closely at the key to her cabin. 'Almost forgot which cabin I'm in,' she said. 'It's B16.'

'Good night, then,' said Knight, who still had a tumbler of whisky before him.

'I'm so sloshed, I've forgotten the cabin number already,' said Marilyn, looking once more at her key. 'Ah yes, it's B16.'

Marilyn departed and Knight gazed through the bar's picture windows at the night sky. A myriad of stars were looking back at him. Should he accept the none-too-veiled invitation to Cabin B16 and whatever adventures awaited him there? Or should he beat a virtuous path back to his own cabin?

Let the Fates decide! He would toss a coin for it. Heads, he would go to Marilyn's cabin. Tails, he wouldn't. Knight spun the coin in the air, caught it in his right hand, and slapped it onto the back of his left hand. Very slowly, he moved his right hand to the side, gradually revealing the face of the coin. It had come down tails.

Knight peered disapprovingly at the coin, then thrust it to the bottom of his pocket. What does a fifty-pence piece know about taking your chances in life, he thought. B16, it is!